I0682930

BODY

&

BLOOD

EDITED BY

WEASEL

Sinister
Stoat
Press

Body & Blood
Vol. 1

EDITOR: Weasel

ISBN-13: 978-1-948712-71-2

Copyright © 2020 Weasel

Cover image and design by Tabsley

All written and visual works remain the sole property of their creators. They are free to use their works however they see fit.

Printed in the U.S.A.

Weasel Press
Lansing, MI
http://www.weaselpress.com

CONTENTS

I first came across erotic horror when I published a novella by Bill Kieffer, *The Goat*—a story that twisted a BDSM relationship into a sick erotic ride. It was a story that made you really evaluate yourself as you read it. It still does.

I had seen sex in horror before, but there was rarely if anything erotic about it. Sex was considered a sin in almost all slasher films. The one thing that will get you killed by the killer. There was nothing yet to make me feel aroused yet horrified at the same time. Clive Barker does it well at times. His writing plays into the reader's desires and twists them painfully. And that's what I was looking for when I started this anthology. I wanted fiction that could deceive the reader, luring them in erotically then slamming them into a dreadfully horrific scene. Some may still be aroused by what they read.

The next rarity for me was queer horror. Horror is a rigid genre, conservative, and it's not often challenged. I wanted to focus on queer authors and queer characters for this project. We don't see them often enough, if at all. The genre has a lot of growth to work on, and being able to challenge the cisgender, straight horror narrative is a necessary yet fun task.

Body & Blood is an anthology that collects queer erotic

horror, and the fiction waiting inside is just eager to tear at you. Do not read carefully. If you're going in, go all in. You might enjoy yourself.

Weasel
The Dude
Sinister Stoat Press

Some of the content in Body & Blood may engage in issues of Homophobia, Dubious Consent, Sexual Assault, Murder, Mental Illness & Ableism, Pornographic content, and transphobic language.

VIII

BODY

&

BLOOD

HOT QUEER WITCHES FIGHT DEMONS
LIA MEYERS

Zo stepped out of the car and took a deep breath of fresh air. Crisp leaves. Fallen apples. Rot and death.

"Do you sense it?" That was Master Grace, already tapping his phone to pull up a photographed spell.

They nodded, glancing at the cabin. Cracked windows stared at them like empty eyes and the door creaked open as if inviting them. "Yes. And I'm ready."

Zo followed their teacher up the gravel driveway and lifted the police tape strung between two trees so that they could duck under.

Master Grace was an older gay man who had discovered his powers to see the paranormal when friends who had died started showing up at his house; he had features as solemn as a basset hound and a slow walk.

This wasn't the first time Zo had followed him into a place of evil—but it was the first time they'd lacked Esther at their side.

Fuck her day job.

Inside the cabin, the air felt different. Colder. Darker. Bleak January rather than September. And there was still blood drying on the peeling linoleum.

Something had caused a perfectly normal group of vacationing teenagers to kill each other. A girl smashed the fireplace poker into her BFF's skull, her boyfriend drowned her in the sink amongst scummy water and broken shards of cheap dishes.

"The evil's coming from—" Zo pointed. "—that back bedroom?" They kept their voice low.

"Correct. Ward yourself and fetch the cursed object; I'll start setting up for the ritual."

They nodded, clutching a fluorite obelisk in the pocket of their cargo pants for comfort as they edged towards the open door.

A waterlogged book stood open on one of the beds. Its pages fluttered, scattering dust; there was no wind.

How could an object with no eyes watch me?

Crazy, but they knew it was staring at them. Waiting. Zo scratched a quick sigil of protection onto their palms and tried to breathe.

If only Esther was here. She'd make a joke about creaky bunk beds, surround herself with a nimbus of power, and walk right up to the cursed artifact. But right now she was safely in Midtown Manhattan, wearing that cute little waitress uniform that hugged her curves, a nametag perched at her ample breasts, wild curls tumbling over her shoulders.

Right. Think of Esther. Don't think of what's inside that book. What you've already seen.

The pages riffled themselves, exposing delicate pen drawings: a man tearing out his own eyeball with long hooked fingernails, a mouse inside a woman's ribcage.

Three steps, and they seized the book.

Boiling oil scalded Zo's hands. Their white fingers convulsed on the worn leather spine as they sprinted back into the main room. Don't let go, don't let go—

"Toss it!" Master Grace shouted, gesturing to the chalk sigils he'd sketched. With an agonized cry, Zo relinquished the book, collapsing just outside the circle. Closed on the ground, it looked so ordinary. Their shaking fingers were mercifully whole.

Acrid mustard-yellow smoke began to seep from between the covers. Its edges blackened.

A necromancer's spirit gaining power to enter reality through the deaths she caused. And if they didn't manage to eradicate her, she would just find a new host, be that object or person.

They had to get it together.

"By the power of these wards, by the purity of amethyst, we bind you, spirit!" Zo managed to say in a loud, clear voice. Fallen leaves and sand orbited them as power rose.

"May you be extinguished like these candles," Master Grace finished. He picked up the white taper candles at the pentacle's points and began pinching them out one by one.

The book's form began to waver, growing insubstantial. It shuddered like a mirage and released more puffs of smoke.

Pressure gripped Zo's head. Something's wrong, they wanted to say. Something is—

Their mouth was full of hair. They leaned forward, retching, spitting. Nothing came out. Hair caressed the inside of their throat, slipped down to strangle their lungs and clench their guts.

The book vanished. The pressure on Zo's head eased; they could breathe again.

Master Grace hurried over. "Are you all right?"

I'm not sure, Zo wanted to say, but what came out was "Absolutely."

"Should we look around and make sure that—"

"Let's go home," they felt their mouth say.

It was like sleep paralysis. Inside, Zo tried desperately to

3

twitch even a finger. Their body moved and smiled, walked back to the car. Their body buckled the passenger side seatbelt as Master Grace began to drive.

Then they yawned. Cold panic filled their mind.

Help me. If I fall asleep, I won't wake up again. Someone else will wear my skin. Push me into an algae-coated lake stagnant by the roadside. Shove salt and vinegar potato chips into my nostrils.

Just please, by Esther's Adonai Hashem and all the saints my ancestors whispered to, don't let me sleep.

Exhaustion suffocated them. They bit the inside of their lip, coaxing blood from the sting.

"That's it. Hush now, little spellcaster." The voice curled around their mind like a contented snake. It was the necromancer's spirit. And she had chosen them to commit their next murder- to bring them back into the world. "Close your eyes and let me see through them. Let your breathing deepen; all the air in your lungs is mine."

They wanted to fight. To lash out. But there was nothing to struggle against, only the car's steady rhythm, this eerie calm.

Esther could make the presence stirring inside of them melt like hot wax, could scratch sigils into their skin until sweet pain helped them breathe. But Esther was half a state away; her tumbling dark curls, her cardamom and jasmine scent. She would have no idea what had happened to Zo.

Another wave of exhaustion threatened to overwhelm them. Even yawning, they felt close to suffocating, chest vise-right under their sports bra.

One final stab at the darkness: Please. Whatever you do to me, don't hurt my Esther.

A sinuous chuckle. "If she is yours, she is mine too. I will devour her magic and leave her to die."

A gasp sucked the last air from their lungs. That laughter followed them into swirling, shivery dreams of collapsing subway tunnels and an endless void.

Decades ago, a ghost-tracker had donated their knuckles to the Order for the Prevention of Necromancy. Touching the wooden box of finger runes always brought Esther a strange comfort.

If a hulking creature with a snake's torso and lion's head licked the flesh from her body with acid and teeth, if she saw beyond the stars at a seance and ripped her own heart out, if she was stuck between the worlds...some fragment of her would live on.

Esther breathed in, breathed out, and tossed the bones.

She had chalked a circle on the kitchen tiles, spread out her Times Square knockoff pashmina in place of a reading cloth.

The bone runes bounced, wobbled, teetered to a stop.

Three were facing up, and she studied the detailed little carvings.

The Exorcism; a femme tied spread-eagled, glittering with tears and diamonds.

The Cloud: catlike eyes peered out from swirls of smoke.

The Treacherous Place: a bridge over a cliff, half rotted away.

Esther sighed. She yanked out her scrunchie and started chewing on her curls. "What are you trying to tell me?"

Her voice sounded uncomfortably loud in the empty apartment. She'd checked the building's wards, and knew they were safe. The symbols on the balcony wind chimes. The points of amethyst under the floorboard. The bags of burnt cinnamon and rusted nails buried around the sidewalk tree below, too deep for an errant dog to touch.

"Esther! What are you doing?"

She swept the bones into a pile and tied the cloth up. "Just meditating. You know, working on my connection with the bones," she said brightly. "How was the bookstore today?"

"The bookstore..." Zo blinked, wrinkling their nose, then

scowled. "Fine." And then, grabbing Esther's arm: "We're going out of the city."

"What? Why?" Something felt off to Esther's magical senses. As if the world had tilted on its axis, Shabbos switched places with Havdalah.

"It's important..." They half-pushed Esther down the stairs, their hand on her back feeling cold as a gun. A car was illegally double-parked outside their apartment, and Zo opened the door. "get in the fucking car, Esther."

"Where are we going?" Esther asked, heart pounding. She fastened her seatbelt as the car drove off.

"Help me," Zo said in a small, quiet voice.

"What?"

Zo shuddered, their hands twitching on the steering wheel. "Shut up and don't ask questions," came out of their mouth. Something was really, really wrong.

Esther had never shut up in her life. She wasn't about to start now. "Are we going to visit my family in New Jersey?"

She was lower east side born and bred, antique mezuzahs on the brownstone, the usual at the kosher deli; Zo, her Zo, would have known that.

Zo, her Zo, had ocean eyes. Coast of California turquoise merperson frolic eyes. The eyes reflected in the rear-view mirror were stoplight warning yellow.

"We're not going to visit your family in New Jersey," the person who was not Zo said distractedly. "We're going... somewhere else."

Esther sank down in her seat and swallowed hard. How could she have been so stupid?

Ever since the cleansing ceremony in the Catskills, Zo had been acting oddly. They popped Esther's gummy vitamins instead of their own neurotransmitters, tiny maracas. They went from curling up to her every night with a seductive grin to sleeping all the way across the bed, arms over their chest like a crusader's statue in a tomb. She'd thought they'd maybe brought some bad energy back, hence the protections on the house.

But Zo hadn't brought anything back.

Zo hadn't come home at all.

An hour or so later, they were in middle-of-nowhere suburbia, the sort of place at the end of a Metro North line. The sort of place where you could scream your lungs out and no one would hear. Not-Zo skidded to a stop on a gravel driveway, shoved the car door open with a burst of psychic energy, and hauled Esther out.

Esther tried to pull away. She could run into the woods, escape. But the stranger's grip was strong.

"Who are you?" she whispered, trying to keep the tremor of terror she felt out of her voice.

"I'm the necromancer who owned this house—the necromancer this body's owner foolishly tried to stop. Come along with me like a good girl, won't you?"

I have no choice, Esther thought with a scowl. But she had her purse with her, and she'd look for an opportunity to use what was inside.

The looming Gothic mansion was all lit up, as if waiting for visitors, but inside, there was a chill in the air, the velvet furniture dusty. Bookshelves lined one wall of the room.

"Sit here, won't you," the necromancer said casually, gesturing to an ornate armchair.

Esther lowered herself into the chair. She focused on breathing deeply and staying calm. "What do you want with us?"

"Killing you will give me the power I need to transform this androgynous body into something more hospitable to my physical desires—and to obliterate anyone who dares stop me." She leaned in with a mocking smile.

Esther drew her head back and slammed it into Zo's—no,

the necromancer's—nose.

With a shriek of anger, she seized Esther's shoulders. Shaking her, trying to slam her head against the wall. Esther lashed out with feet and knees until she could leap from the chair, but the necromancer tackled her. They went down rolling, punching; Esther tried to draw her witch-knife, but it was knocked out of her hand and bounced away across the carpet. With a desperate lunge, she gripped the hilt. As the necromancer scrambled atop her, she lashed out, hitting her hard in the stomach.

It hurt to see Zo curled up in pain, wincing with every breath.

This wasn't Zo anymore, Esther reminded herself, weighing the knife's balance, squeezing it to activate the runes—

"Esther," Zo sobbed, and Esther hesitated, the tension ebbing from her raised fist. Zo—and this time it was Zo, their teary eyes tropical blue again—struggled to sit up, clutching at Esther's blouse.

"Esther, please. You mustn't let go of me. It's me, I promise."

More than anything, she wanted to believe that her Zo was back. Was safe. But she'd been trained too well. "What are you getting me for our four-year anniversary?"

"We decided we were counting from when we met, it's our fifth—"

When Esther let out a relieved breath, Zo clutched tighter. "Esther, if you leave me now, if you stop holding my hand, I may not be able to find my way back."

"It's really you," Esther stammered, drawing them into her arms. Zo even smelled normal again, and she soaked up the familiar scent.

Zo nodded weakly. "Mostly me. I'm...struggling. Esther, I'm so sorry—I would have done anything to—"

"Tell me what I need to know now. You can tell me how much you love me later."

"There's a memory-warded safe somewhere in this room, a

book inside— nngh! It belonged to the necromancer. A failsafe for all her spells, just in case she needed to keep someone alive. It lured you here to kill you and burn the house, burn your body. Get rid of all that could destroy it. The safe's not fireproof. Neither are you—" They shuddered, color draining from their skin. "God. Esther, forget it. We don't have time. Set the place on fire with me inside if you have to."

Nothing could make me give up on you, Esther wanted to say, I promised I'd spend the rest of my life with you, and if that bitch tries to destroy you they'll have to go through me first—

But there wasn't time. Instead she tangled her fingers in Zo's short hair and kissed them with all the passion and love in her body; they were hers and warm and real, and kissing her back desperately.

I would die for this, she thought. I'd die for you.

When Zo pulled away abruptly, they weren't Zo. Their eyes were yellow. A warning.

Esther wouldn't back down.

"Enjoyed your last kiss goodbye?" the necromancer teased, with a smile that showed inhuman teeth.

"Come at me," Esther taunted.

The necromancer tried to stand—but Zo's arm was handcuffed to the sturdy armchair's leg. Esther had used the distraction to slip the handcuffs from her purse.

A sneer twisted those handsome features. "This won't hold me for long." Already the metal was starting to smoke yellow.

"It doesn't matter," Esther said, sounding more confident than she felt. She closed her eyes and patted the books on the shelves. One had a different energy signature; no one had ever flipped through its pages. When she pulled the book, a nearby section of wall swung open, revealing a safe.

Hmm. No visible lock. Still, as she hovered her palm a few inches from the metal, magic shivered against her skin.

"You have seen a memory lock before, haven't you? Enjoy

reliving your worst moments."

"I don't have any bad memories. I've lived a happy life full of victories, and this will be just one more."

But when she touched the lock, she sensed it was warded by demon magic. Its power was snaking into her thoughts, taking her back to the past...and re-writing her memories.

Esther reported to the New York Society headquarters to assist in her first demon banishment at precisely midnight, but she hadn't expected there would be another trainee sitting in on the process. This smug LA bleach-blonde hipster had an answer to everything and the cockiest smirk.

Every time Esther hesitated with an answer, they'd say something like, "Umm, actually, I've gone over that with my coven," or "You did do the reading, right?"

Their mohawk reminded Esther of a cockatoo; they wore a perfectly ironed linen shirt and flawlessly highlighted cream contour. It could have been some Ashkenazi ancestral memory responding to tall blue-eyed blondes with an immediate Nope, or just the way they subtly looked Esther's waitress uniform up and down, but she didn't like them.

When it came time to ground and center, rooting energy into the earth and drawing power up, they barely closed their vivid eyes before announcing "Done." And when it came time to invoke the element of fire in the circle, they lit the braided candle Esther had brought with a single snap.

Shit. A lifetime of Kabbalah and the craft and she'd never manage the showy flourishes that this skinny David Bowie knockoff produced effortlessly.

Then the unexpectedly strong demon had ripped through her master's shields like so much wet tissue paper, and they'd barely managed to find refuge in a closet on the second floor.

As the demon's footsteps shook the floor, they huddled together amidst mops and grimoires.

"What should we do?"

Esther's training came back to her in the darkness. "If we work together, we might be able to surprise it with a banishing spell."

Then claws tore through the door.

Inside Esther's mind, the demon lock whispered.

(How could you expect to work magic together? You'd only just met. Your energy jangled out of tune and harsh, contrasting colors that muddied and burned.)

Zo, horror in their ocean eyes as high-pressure blood fountained out of their nose, dirtying the grimy tiles. They sank to their knees. Blood seeped through their jeans. But they didn't care. There wasn't enough Zo left in their body to care at all—

Esther fought as hard as she could, dredging up specific sensory impressions she could use as a shield. Peanut butter cookies still warm from the oven, melting in her mouth. Sheets fresh out of the dryer. The taut cotton of Zo's bra. She was shaking. But she tugged the memory back onto its real path.

She'd turned to Zo: "You okay?"

"I'm sorry. I'm really nervous. And you know so much more magic than I do, you're so much better at grounding and centering—fuck, I've been a total bitch. If we can't banish the demon together, just ward yourself and let me die."

A feeling of protectiveness and fury surprised her with its flaring intensity. "Never. The society doesn't do that. I won't do that. I won't leave you, Los Angeles."

"My name is—"

The demon was getting closer, big footsteps thumping on the tiles. Esther shushed them. "Tell me if we live."

Their magic had blended in an intense swirl of power, breathtaking unison and shimmering strength.

A few hours later, they were seated on the building's stoop, watching Master Grace describe the incident to higher-ups. "Please tell me this isn't how apprentice training rituals usually go," they said, half-laughing.

"Oh, fuck no. This demon just found a new way of eluding the power-assessment charm, is all. Made it look like a little imp suitable for training on when he was actually super big and dangerous. But usually there's a lot less almost death. What's your name?"

"Zo. And I'm actually from San Francisco. How would you like it if I started calling you Jersey?"

"Ouch. Point taken." She took a deep breath. "Hey, this is going to sound ridiculous, but..."

Cool interest flickered deep in those turquoise eyes. "Yeah?"

"Would you maybe want to go to Insomnia Cookies with me? They're open. Hot cookies straight out of the oven."

"I do have a major sweet tooth." From the way they looked at Esther and smiled slow and easy, her instincts sensed they were talking about more than just cookies.

A few hours later, they were in her apartment; "come and see my crystal collection" had turned into "I really, really want to kiss you right now" and a frantic tumble into bed.

Esther had been kissing her way down Zo's stomach, but she lifted her head. "I don't usually do this on the first date," she said breathlessly.

Zo smirked, that expression Esther would've wanted to slap if it didn't make them look so fuckable; they were reclining on Esther's beaded pillows like a reigning monarch. "Hey, I sure as hell don't mind."

Esther pulled her hand back from the metal. She was breathing hard; her skin felt sensitive and tight, nipples pressing against her unpadded bra. "First lock."

"But there's still one more. And this one's stronger," promised the necromancer.

No, Esther thought. *I am*. She stroked circles around the cool, smooth safe until the magic sucked her in.

Rain over the forest. Wood smoke. Pinecones crackling

in an absinthe-green fire. The witch lived in the Pine Barrens, stewing rumors of the Jersey Devil to entrap the curious. A scraping sound on a camp window: not a monster's claws, only her filleting knives before she scooped campers from their beds and skinned them alive.

Remember what happened next, the memory spell whispered. Maybe they loved you, but this is when you lost them. When your spells failed.

Esther collapsed to the floor, carpet bruising their knees. She'd thought they were dealing with a demon, and she'd crept around the burnt pines and marshy mud for hours setting a trap as Zev raced over sand and blacktop and snapping twigs, using herself as distraction and bait. But it wasn't a demon, and that dark magic crackled through Zo's body worse than a police taser. You watched the witch shave their sun-and-straw hair, then take the razor to their skin, opening all the long-forgotten cuts hatred had made, and their eyes went dead before their heartbeat stopped—

Sunlight slanting through the trees. Cool metal under her bare ass. The sensory impressions of what had truly happened were too strong. Esther dialed up reality and wore truth like a blanket cloak.

When the trap failed, I had my knife.

"Just in case it isn't a demon," Zo said, pressing it into my hand. I rolled my eyes and chuckled but I still had it in my belt. Dim cloudy sunlight on the basil-oiled blade. She swung her staff; I stumbled back.

I tripped over broken ferns and rotting branches. I knew I would die. Then Zev darted out from the blackberry thorns, undercut shining like white fire. "Hey, witch bitch! You want a human sacrifice? Take me. My eyes will be tastier than hers ever could. I have more power. I've seen so much more."

The witch stabbed them with the broomstick, shooting

dark energy through their vulnerable body. With a cry, they collapsed to the leaf litter.

I found my knife where it had fallen. Found my footing, silent as a wildcat. And then I struck.

The delicious memory continued to unspool. They set a ward around the cottage so nothing else would burn, dragged the dismembered bodies into the lake where they might still be found by mortal hands, and limped past the fire. Blood pounding in their hearts, blood still safe inside their bodies. In this moment the sheer joy of life was a truth that could never be changed, and they kissed again and again.

"Your body is the safest place I know," Zo whispered, pulling away to lean their foreheads together. "So brave, so soft—I really want to be inside you right now, and I've got a strap-on in my car."

"Why do you have a—"

"I was a pegging instructor at kink camp. Before I forget how the buckles work; fuck, Esther, you have no idea what you do to me. Feel my heart racing."

She put her hand on their chest.

"That's my tits," Zo pointed out.

"I know," Esther said with a wink. "I like feeling those too."

Zo chuckled and nuzzled her neck.

Esther ended up helping them with the buckles, and then kneeling in the dew-wet grass to take all seven inches of silicone into her mouth. The broken, whimpering noises Zo made as they struggled to keep standing were better than any chant of a successful spell, any whoosh of enchantment-lit flames. She ended up naked over the hood of Zo's mint-green vintage Mustang, jean skirt and tights around her ankles as the silicone cock plunged into her, a welcome invasion with every thrust. Her sweaty ass stuck to the car, and she could feel every scratch in the metal. Every ridge on the cock.

Zo's face when their eyes fluttered closed and they finally smiled was as bright as the cool autumn dawn, and she wrapped her legs around them, taking them deeper, deeper still—

A scream of rage echoed in her head as the seal broke. She wanted to slap her hands over her ears and run, but she took a deep breath and pulled the safe open. Inside was a worn parchment book, the cover engraved with a pentacle. Bits of ribbon and leaf pressed into service as bookmarks stuck out the sides.

The necromancer was shrieking now, tugging furiously at the handcuffs.

"You stupid bitch! You'll never—"

"Yeah, sure, okay," Esther called back as she ran into the next room. The necromancer had probably never used this absurdly fancy living room; a blanket of dust fell over the glittering crystal sculptures, and deep velvet drapes flowed over the walls. She was the only real, living human who'd crossed its threshold, and took an odd pleasure in defiling it with her vibrant life as she sprawled out on the carpet and quickly read.

Finally she found the spell she wanted. The spell required chalk, incense, and three quartz stones of varying size, all basic charm ingredients she kept in her purse.

Breathe, she told herself, hastily stripping out of her long-sleeved shirt and denim maxi, her pretty lace bralette and matching undies. Think of Zo's eyes, their hands. The soft secret wetness under those boxer shorts. That face they make when they're trying to stave off an orgasm for a few more moments, like an anguished angel. Their contented little smirk afterwards, like nothing will ever bother them again.

Esther rubbed the first smooth tumbled stone across her clit, the power it contained buzzing low in her belly. The second quartz she licked all over, caressing it with her tongue; the third and largest, a weighty egg shape, she slipped into her cunt. Its wide shape was a stretch, but when she withdrew it, all she craved was deeper and more. Pinching and stroking her nipples, letting the tense fear ebb from her body under a slow onslaught of pleasure, Esther knew the spell was building—and so was her orgasm. But knowing that Zo needed her, it was easy to resist the urge to stroke her pulsing cunt. To channel all that energy and want and need into the spell.

Naked and fearless, she strode back into the sitting room, where she laid the three glistening rocks around the struggling necromancer.

"You foolish child. You don't know what you're doing. I could give you unlimited power!"

"I don't want unlimited power. I want my partner back," Esther said calmly, setting the incense aflame.

"Sentimental, aren't you? I could help you find a new partner. A magically stronger one." Her voice was lower now, seductive, eyes half-lidded in languorous invitation.

Esther didn't want Zo's body with this stranger inside—she wanted Zo worshipping her, taking refuge within her. As she chanted, each liquid syllable hung in the air. A soap bubble, a glimmering ornament, crowding the room with shivers of light. The tentatively forming spell trembled against her body, a soft fluttering pressure; her voice faltered, but she chanted on. Steady thrumming between her legs matched a racing heartbeat as she sped towards the end of the spell, breath coming in quick gasps.

"You don't know what you're doing—you don't know what I could give you—"

Shut up, Esther thought, and curled her lips around the last hefty syllable, a hiss that shot straight through the air—

Pleasure exploded like a firework as power poured from their body in pulsing, molten cascades. She could hear herself laughing, the necromancer's anguished cries; when at last the world steadied, she caught her breath.

Zo stirred, moaning faintly. When their eyes fluttered open, they were bright blue again.

Holy fuck, thank Hashem..."Hey, baby," Esther said, her voice shaking as she tried to rearrange Zo's fauxhawk into its usual perfect coif. She loved the familiar texture of their bleach-fried hair. "How are you feeling?"

Zo released the handcuffs and rubbed their wrists. "Pretty good. My head's a little spinny, but.." Then they noticed that Esther was naked, their gaze deliberately zoning in on her breasts. "Strike that. I'm great. Really great. Come lie here on the carpet with me?"

Esther stretched out next to them; unexpectedly, Zo pulled her close. "Do you have any idea how much it turns me on? Seeing you wield all that power, so calm and strong and focused, with that intense look in your eyes—I want you so much right now."

"In the house where you were possessed by a demon? You could have died here. I've missed you so much, missed touching you...but you don't have to have sex to prove you're still you."

Zo shook their head, curling around Esther with gentle touches that felt exquisite on her spell-sensitized skin. "I was wandering in a desert at night. No moon, no stars, just endless grey sand. Wherever I went, nothing but death and desolation. Then I felt your hands on my shoulder and I was back in my body—I had a body. You helped me remember I was real, and just being able to breathe felt amazing." They clutched her shoulders, desperation shimmering in their eyes. "I want to get used to having control over my own limbs for a few days before you fuck me but give me something to do with my mouth besides think about what I've just been through. Let me make you feel that good."

"Of fucking course," Esther murmured, understanding softening her resistance. After all, she was still incredibly aroused from the working she'd just completed. She ended up against the wall, Zo's hands on her hips while they ate her out. Their tongue stroked over her wet folds with exquisite gentleness; teasing, arousing, giving pleasure space to build once more.

Zo pulled back, grinning, and licked their lips. "I can taste the magic on your body."

"What's it like?"

"Like sea salt. Like roses."

She laughed, but tugged on Zo's hair. "Stop talking and lick me, you absolute poet."

Zo happily did. They smelled like wood smoke and hairspray and sweat, their bleached hair stiff as Esther dug her fingernails into their scalp, yanking their mouth to exactly where she wanted it as her impending orgasm gained strength. She could feel the power moving through them both, flickering, rising like a flame.

I love you, she thought—I love, I love— Light burst around them, an explosion flaring loud inside her head. The aurora borealis dazzled her sight.

When she awoke, she was propped up on the sofa. It was broad daylight; outside the sparrows flew between the oaks. Zo sat beside her, talking into their cellphone.

"Yes, I'll file a mission report; I don't think the ritual Esther used would be appropriate for general order-wide distribution, seeing as it's entirely reliant on owning a vulva, but I'll make a clean copy in a fresh Book of Shadows nevertheless—hold on a second." They muted the call. "Hey, Esther-mine. That was a lot of power moving through you. How are you feeling?"

She stretched, enjoying the satisfied sensations of her well-tended body. "Amazing. I wouldn't mind a few more hours of sleep, unless you want to drive back home?"

They caressed Esther's torso, fingertips warm through the woven blanket. "Wherever we spend the weekend, I'm fine with it. My home is right here."

A DESPERATE MISSIVE
YSADORA ALEXANDER

You have asked me time and time again to recount the tale of the Moth-Man. I must admit Edward, I cannot tell the awful tale in person, instead I shall include it in this missive. Cowardly? I suppose so, but there is something in the telling of this arduous horror that is almost paralyzing to the mind. I shall try my best, please do not feel that this is in some way dismissive of your interest on the subject, but merely an internal failing on my own part.

Forgive me.

I met Lord Emmanuel Mothe on the 21st of January 1882. He was a learned man of sharp intellect and fine clothes. Ever so charismatic, he held salons, and spoke for many hours each time to an utterly enthralled audience. The topics of such meets ranged widely, from metaphysics to theology, ancient history to contemporary art analyses. He was a verbal artist, a word smith of the highest order.

When he looked at me, I felt as though he saw into my very soul. His gaze was entrancing, making me feel as though he was noticing me, comprehending me, like no other had before. Or would ever again. By the sighs and swoons around the room, others were clearly feeling this effect, both men and women alike.

I fancy that I was rather unique, however, as it was me, and me alone who he approached after delivering a rousing speech upon the symbiotic relationship between the creative and the insane within one mind. It was a darkened evening in May of that year, if I do recall, however due to the events that occurred thereafter, I cannot be sure of the date. Truth be told, I cannot be sure of even the month, although my ladies' companion noted a marked change in my demeanor around that time, so I have deduced that it must have been then.

No intoxicant nor opiate substance I have consumed since has managed to produce the same effect on my manner, although I have sought it again and again. I suppose I am trying to replicate the euphoria, without the horror. But I digress, and have fallen to rambling. No Edward, this will not do.

Lord Mothe came to me, and all eyes followed. He smiled, a beautiful smile, opened his beautiful mouth.

"Do you understand the nature of moths?"

I confessed to only knowing of their transformations. He smiled, and stated that he would call on me again, before returning to his guests.

A kind of mania followed this simple interaction. I became possessed by the need to research every piece of information I could find pertaining to moths, from the common white moth, to the myriad brown moths that habitually haunted our woodland areas. I began a collection, obtaining rare species such as the giant leopard, the flame brocade and even the death's head hawk-moth, Acherontia atropos. I commissioned a beautiful set of drawers, protecting my treasures in every stage of their life cycle. We cannot have the moth without the larva.

The time came for another of Lord Mothe's salons, a treatise on the requirement of higher education in the interests of evolution. I readied myself, donning a grand red brocade gown with a gilt moth pin fastened at the bodice. My companion, sensing my keenness and knowing the nature of my recent forays into entomology begged me not to attend. She stated that she had some kind of psychical turn, and had sensed evil was afoot. I merely dismissed her and her foolishness. Oh Edward, if only I had listened.

Arriving at the grand manor of Lord Mothe, I was ushered in with the others in a very secretive manner. So much so, that many of us became greatly ill at ease. Contrary to previous events, this time there was a single table in the center of the room. It was large, set for a full 20 seated persons. We milled around, none too willing to venture into this anomaly. As Lord Mothe entered the room in grand form, we were all compelled to sit at once, his enchantment upon us. This night, he announced, there would be no noble treatise. In its place he was holding a grand séance, lead by a feeble old woman from the Society of Psychical Research. Lord Mothe believed that that the greater the number involved in the séance, the greater the results would be. He had deduced that the number of attendees at his salons would suffice to produce physical manifestations.

Many of those around me began to visibly pale and sweat, although none stood to leave. I wish I could tell you of grand things that night, Edward dear, but truthfully, we had no success at all. No emanations, no spirits, no bloodied relics. The pale hag implored the spirits repeatedly to make an appearance, but it was in vain. The briefest flicker of annoyance crossed Lord Mothe's normally serene countenance, but it was soon replaced by his usual polite facade. One by one we all stood, preparing to leave.

Lord Mothe came to me again.

"Do you understand the nature of moths?"

I was prepared, regaling him with scientific names, statistics, and lists of their most desirable features. He smiled politely as he listened, but as soon as I paused to take a breath, he eloquently excused himself. He left promising he would call on me again.

The melancholy was all consuming, upon reaching my small home I became enraged, destroying all crockery within my reach. I was not to be dissuaded however and plunged myself deeper into my research. I became a regular patron of the library, consuming every tome they had on the subject of my ardor. At length I interrogated a scientist on the matter, one who had dedicated his life to the study of nocturnal insects. So much so that he had become nocturnal himself. My extensive knowledge on the subject impressed him greatly, and he pondered the nature of my fascination. I reassured him that it was merely a passing fancy, that I had no designs on taking up employment in the field. For my own dignity I could not divulge that it was to ingratiate myself to Lord Emmanuel Mothe. That would not do for a proud woman of good family such as myself.

After bearing witness to the séance, I deduced that he may be looking for a more metaphysical approach. Thus I sought out witches, mystics and all manner of cunning men and women, capable of furnishing my many questions with answers. Studying the symbology of the moth consumed my entire being. Omens of death and disaster, a sign of the heretic as well as messages from the deceased all abounded.

In time I deduced that the humble moth had rather negative connotations for the human psyche.

Eagerly I awaited the next of Lord Mothe's gatherings, checking each day if an invitation had arrived from his manservant. Each day brought another disappointment, another mournful moment, my companion gazing at me with concern clouding her doe eyes. I lost great amounts of weight due to my obsession, a pallid complexion only broken by my dark sunken eyes became my daily mask. My death mask. On I waited until fear emboldened me. I dressed in my finest, all black brocade, lace and velvet. Hair curled and pinned, a touch of arsenic to take the yellow from my face. As thus I travelled to the home of Lord Mothe unbidden, a mighty taboo for a woman such as myself. His servants displayed a distaste at my audacity as I awaited the lord in a small drawing room, seemingly reserved for uncalled upon guests it seems. It was suitably uncomfortable and unpleasant.

There I waited, polishing the silver buckles of my shoes on my stockings, preening mindlessly to soothe my nerves. In time the door was thrown open and Lord Mothe strode into the room.

"Do you understand the nature of moths?"

I was ready. Moths transform, and are exotic creatures found around the world in many different forms, it is true. Only a moth however, lives as a creature of the day, then transforms into a creature of the night, embraced by darkness as it was once embraced by the sun.

Lord Mothe paused a moment, before breaking out into an ecstatic smile. Yes, moths transform into a creature of darkness and the mire. Much like I had become, with my skeletal form and air of malaise.

Dear Edward, it was then I was caught in his trap.

Lord Mothe took my hand in his, leading me through a warren of halls and dizzying turns. At length we stood on the threshold of a dark door, wrought from pure iron. The preceding hall had no decoration nor egress, unbroken by any aperture at all. He grinned maniacal, unlatching the heavy door with a complex key suspended from a chain around his neck. He held my shoulders, his eyes burning down into mine in such an intoxicating manner. Desire shrouded my greater judgement, I cared not for what lay beyond that forbidding portal.

"Are you sure you wish to continue?"

The door was thrown open, well-greased hinges belied its weighty exterior. Beyond, when my eyes adjusted to the gloom, lay something of a laboratory. A laboratory with an enormous looking glass, an exquisite gilded mirror before a great bed. A heavy sewing machine sat in the corner, littered with pieces of pale leather, which for some reason I was loathe to touch. Lord Mothe bounded into the room, gesturing that I must sit upon the bed. I complied with some trepidation, despite a growing sense of dis-ease. I even allowed him to cover my eyes with a blindfold of his own design. The darkness was absolute, representative of the pupae stage he explained. I could hear Lord Mothe busying himself around the room, preparing some great surprise to reveal to me when the blindfold arose.

I waited dutifully, listening to the rustlings, openings, and closings. In time Lord Mothe announced he was ready, and I pulled off the blinder. The horror before me was only realized after long moments of gazing in confusion of what I perceived. Lord Emmanuel Mothe en-robed in the costume of a moth. This was no ordinary entomological ensemble, but one lovingly crafted from flesh. The more I stared, paralyzed with terror, the more was revealed to me. The torso was patch-worked with hair of different tones, still attached to the scalp and trimmed to a uniform length. The wings were sewn from skin in various hues, with an array of nipples forming the various spots adorning a moth's appendages. I gaped in awe, unwillingly taking in all I saw before me.

There he stood before me, in all his glory, the macabre moth man. A terrible, beautiful grin spread across his face as he gazed down upon me. I spluttered and stammered, unsure of what to say, or if he intended my husk to join his apparel. His bright demeanor dimmed slightly as his wings drooped. I stood and forced a smile, promising to call upon him. Thus I fled, wending my way through the labyrinthine halls. I do not know how I managed to negotiate my way through to the front door, but I ran from the manor. When I reached the threshold of my abode, I realized that I still clutched to the blindfold. Opening my hand, I saw that it too had been made from flesh, and two nipples made up the eyes. Pupal indeed!

I have since quit my home in the city, absconding for the countryside loft in which I now reside. All ties there are cut, save for my companion and your good self. Please Edward, please I implore you. Send help. Every moth that flutters around my lamp, every beaten wing against my window...I am haunted.

ROSES BLOOM AT NIGHT
TAMARA WERTEEN

I'm trying to decide if the florist is helping because I'm a hot mess, or because I'm messy hot. She's carrying herself with a raw, lonely kind of beauty. Long auburn hair, old-soul blue eyes. Freckles.

Constellations mapping the universe on her skin.

She's cute. I try to remember Vanessa's warning as I gape at her dimpled cheek, the exact wording a poorly veiled condemnation of my plan to visit *Roses Bloom at Night* to pick out a houseplant for my sister's apartment warming.

"It's trés creepy, Samantha. People go in but don't always come out." Vanessa said, licking the whip off the tip of her reusable metal straw. Whether it had been her moist, pink tongue or the fact she'd paid 8 dollars for a coffee, I'd been too distracted to really listen to her as she side-eyed me and rambled on. I'd finally focused as she said "Just go to WalMart, everything is cheaper there. And nobody disappears from Wally-world."

"You read too many online gossip rags, Vanessa." I felt my cheeks grow warm as she expertly applied lip gloss post sugary treat. "Plus, I think that's the plot to some cult-fav horror movie. The one where they sing about Seymour?"

She'd pouted bubblegum glossed lips and rolled her eyes. "Don't say I didn't warn you."

We'd collected our books, cram session for finals officially concluded as her phone jingled a 7 p.m. alarm. She hugged me briefly, full, pert breasts brushing against my flat chest on the sidewalk before entering her uber. I headed out on foot as she waved goodbye, intending to hoof it home in my battered adidas.

I daydreamed as I walked, relatively safe in this neighborhood. Any leering males were usually dissuaded by my tomboy figure. It was hard to make a girl feel dirty about curves that didn't exist.

Tripping over the uneven sidewalk had interrupted my reimagining of Vanessa's flicking tongue and wondering what color her bra was. My arms had pinwheeled wildly, ill-fated trajectory leading me to clutch the nearest lamp post for support before I found myself in the street.

"Fuck!" I'd muttered shakily, forcing myself to collect my pride and look up from my sneakers.

I'd somehow wandered myself to a near death experience just outside the single-story florist shop in question. Faded green paint peeled from the trim as a dull neon sign flickered "open, open, open" in the dying light. The clock sign in the window read "Come in!" with two hands declaring I had just ten minutes to make the welcome bell jingle. Someone had painted the smiley face into a sunflower.

Teapot roses were arranged in the window in a pyramid display, the healthiest of which was blood red. My sister's favorite color.

I'd mustered my courage and pulled the ancient wrought iron handle toward me, entering into the dim shop lighting. Inside smelled of flora and earth, and I'd turned to examine the display in the window. The sun had just dipped below the roofs across the street, and I'd squinted as my eyes adjusted to the light.

My sister's crimson beauty had been perched mid display just behind a hand lettered piece of cardboard that read "Ask Lola for help, we bite!".

I'd glanced around, decided Lola must be in the back, and reached toward the display.

"Sorry the roses were being...pricks." There's a halting lilt to the joke. I can hear the unspoken question there. Her voice is smooth caramel. Her fingers are lingering longer than necessary on mine.

Her wink indicates her vote is for messy-hot. Most definitely.

My uninjured hand brushes unruly blonde curls from my face. I chew my lip. Pretend the flush in my cheeks is from the startled jump I gave when the thorn had pricked my finger. I've knocked a dozen rose bushes to the floor in a cacophonous crash. Become lightheaded at the bead of blood growing on my thumb.

This ethereal woman, "Hi, I'm Lola!" pinned to her partially buttoned blouse, had dashed from the back at the sound of shattering pots, finding me the cause of her alarm.

I've stopped her from closing up shop. The streetlights are flickering on outside.

Embarrassing.

Her hand is still holding mine. Pleasant heat takes root in my lower abdomen under the floral rainbow illuminated by humming fluorescent lights. I formulate my response.

"No worries. Every rose has its thorn." A spatter of my blood has dripped on her white tile floor. We both avoid eye contact by watching it congeal. She's still holding the tissue to my skin.

I let her.

"I'll find my 'slippery when wet' sign?" She suggests bravely. I snort with laughter. She's reading my body language as inviting. Her thumb brushes my palm. I shiver.

This is much different from the time Danny had fumbled with my bra strap after prom. I'd let him touch me and more in the backseat of his mother's Honda Civic. It had been a cold, lifeless act. I'd found the sun-faded "little tree" air freshener to be more entertaining than the grunting going on in my ear. I'd survived, knowing the task had to be done sooner or later. How else would I have ever answered the question that had been burning inside of me since ninth grade gym class, all of those naked bodies in matching bra and panty sets making me doubt my sanity?

I pull back from her hand, shocked at this instant attraction to her. It reminded me of the shame I felt years ago as a dozen girls I'd never talk to again had begun whispering about my staring.

She misinterprets. Lets go of my hand with a sigh.

The tissue falls.

I grab her wrist. Catch my breath. Wet my lips. "Roses just became my favorite flower."

Now it's her turn to blush and she flips the open sign to closed. Her eyes burn into mine as she draws the shades. Locks the door.

The fallen rose bushes crush gently under her sandaled feet as she tugs me toward her. I'm encompassed by the heady aroma of their released oils and her shampoo. Warm summer and green apples.

I'm finding it hard to breath, her lips soft petals over blunt teeth nibbling at my neck. I hold her shoulders and arch my neck back to grant her better access. A cool, slim hand slithers under my shirt to my unsupported breasts. Her fingernails tease their peaks.

I can't focus on the shop and the feeling her hands have awakened inside of me. My eyes flutter shut. I gasp.

Each flick sends a shockwave through me, and I tremble as she unbuttons my pants. Slides them down.

Something tickles my knee, I brush it away. It returns, more insistent. Something pricks me. Once. Twice. Then a burning rake up my delicate inner thigh to the core of me, and I'm torn from ecstasy by pain. I look down to identify the source of my sudden agony. Lola is holding a rose bush, dirt pattering from it's naked roots to the floor. It's the one I'd picked for my sister.

She grins, her grip moving to tighten in my hair. There is deep malice in that smile and an empty cavernous terror fills me. I jerk my hands up to push her away. She holds my blonde curls captive.

Her voice no longer sounds like caramel, sweet, syrupy, warm. Now she sounds of wet gravel road crunching in my ear.

"The sign says they bite. You should have asked for help."

Her hand twists in my hair. Yanks my head with inhuman force. My neck is shattered in an instant. The heat from my skin, the touch of her hands, gone. My mind is screaming panicked alarms, but my body is an unfeeling lump as I collapse to the floor amid the potting soil and clay shards. The angle of my ruined spine allows me to observe her perfectly as continues in her violation of me.

She's on top of me, moving, panting, writhing and moaning pleasure I've never allowed myself to experience. I helplessly watch her with my unblinking stare as she forces the entire rose bush into my womanhood before ripping it out. Thorns and stems gouge my flesh, but I feel nothing as my blood pools there, staining the greenery crimson with each intrusion. Her freckles appear darker against the flush growing on her cheeks.

Stars gone out. Black holes. The abyss.

Mercifully, my vision begins to fade, neurons unable to continue normal function. Before it can go dark, I see her reach

into the coagulating pool between the carnage of my legs.
She gathers blood and torn rose petals in cupped hands.
Turns to the remaining potted plants.
And feeds it drop by drop into their soil.
One faded image comes to me as the final darkness shrouds
my mind.
An air freshener hanging from a rearview mirror.
A faded little tree.

THE FALL
WILLIAM HOLDEN

Sean stood in the bathroom doorway. The steam from the shower engulfed him as rivulets of water trickled down his back and chest. A puddle of cooling water gathered at his feet while he waited, unable to step into the bedroom. Ghosts lingered in the darkness, and he had many of them. *Acceptance is the first step in recovery.* A voice, not quite unknown to him, echoed in his mind. He now kept the light on a timer, so it always came on as the light of the day died. An icy finger brushed across the nape of his neck. A breath caught in his throat. The light timer clicked illuminating the bedroom in a soft, white glow.

The covers on his bed were the way he left them that morning, tossed to one side and wrinkled. His pillows mangled beneath the twists and clumps of sheets. His flannel blue-green plaid boxers hung from the bedpost. Everything was a reminder of another moment lost to time.

Beneath the lamp, a framed photograph of him and his late husband, Neal. Sean stepped across the threshold and into the bedroom. He smiled with the memories of their honeymoon in Paris. A short year ago, and now all that remained were memories and even those seemed to be fading. There were moments when he couldn't remember being in Paris. Yet, there they were with the Eiffel Tower rising behind them. All that remained was him, and the ghosts of the accident, which left his husband dead.

Sean's body shivered despite the hot August night. The antique clock—his great grandfathers—struck eight from the fireplace mantel. Each note echoed through the apartment with its slow, deep bong. He took a step closer toward the bed and stretched out his hand. Grasping the boxers between the tips of two fingers, he slipped them over his body. The soft, worn material was a small comfort, but one he welcomed.

He looked down at his feet. He wiggled his toes against the cool wood floors. The darkness seemed to slither out from under the bed, inching its way toward him. The light cutting across the floorboards kept the shadows at bay. He jumped onto the bed and pulled the covers over his body before the darkness could get any closer. The lampshade wiggled making shadows dance across the surface of the walls and ceiling.

Sean wanted to turn off the light. To exterminate the shadows, but he knew the darkness would bring the ghosts. They would stand around the bed, watching him sleep. They would snicker and tease him and chase away any chance of rest. Sean turned his back on the light and closed his eyes. Using the ticking clock as his anchor, he let himself drift to sleep.

The black of the night surrounded Sean as he laid in bed and stared at the ceiling he knew was there but couldn't see. There was something in the room with him. He couldn't see it. He couldn't hear it. He felt it. There was a presence in the room with him and it had turned off the light leaving him defenseless.

Sean in a desperate act of survival reached his hand into the darkness. He patted the nightstand then let his fingers walk up the base of the lamp. Fumbling for the switch, he turned it. Nothing happened. He tried again in reverse. The light was dead.

Panic ripped through his body. "Please, not again." He begged the darkness as his mind tried to grab onto a safety line —the voice. *Try to focus on something real, Sean. No matter where you are. Keep yourself grounded and don't let go. Remember it's all in your mind. Nothing in the fall is real. It's the manifestation of your subconscious.*

"Come on, Sean. Focus." It was then that he heard it. The complete and utter silence. The clock was no longer ticking away the seconds. Time became eternal, unable to count or track. The central air was no longer humming. He couldn't even hear his heart drumming in his ears or feel the blood pulsing through his body. "Please, leave me alone." He whispered to the darkness. The all too familiar weight settled onto his chest. It pressed and squeezed until a burning ache seized each breath. He began to fall.

Panic spread throughout Sean's body. Its tendrils snaked their way through his veins in an attempt to control his movement. He gripped the sheets hoping it would be enough to keep him grounded. The soft, comforting fabrics were no longer there. Instead, his fingers slid through the nothingness of the fall.

The fear of the unknown was too much for Sean to bear. He opened his eyes. His mattress had become a damp bed of moss and grass, his room the all too familiar cemetery. The hair on his chest, damp with pre-dawn dew, shimmered with the caress of the moon's final touch.

The graveyard stretched out on all sides. Rolling hills of manicured grass reached out into the dark horizon. Thousands of headstones rose above the well-maintained lawn and looked like gray liver spots set against emerald-green skin. A morbid curiosity sank into his thoughts as he looked around from the strange vantage point. *Is this how it looks when you're dead?* The terrifying thought drifted through the fog in his mind. A coldness settled against his feet. He rubbed his toes against the smooth, chilled surface of the headstone. He read the inscription for the umpteenth time, though it felt as if it was the first. *Neal Parker. Born October 1, 1975–August 3, 2018. Beloved Son and Husband.*

The ground shifted. Sean held his breath and waited, wondering if he imagined it. Then, a sound, so quiet, so faint he wasn't sure it was a sound at all. He listened. Something or someone was digging beneath him. The soil moved. His body sank. Without warning, the earth opened and swallowed him.

The overturned soil sprayed across his face and mouth. He choked on the foul-tasting dirt as he clawed at the edge of the grave and tried to hold on. The force was too strong. Hands, cold, dead, invisible reached around his body and pulled him farther into the hole. Closer to his husband's corpse. Dirt and grass filled his fingernails as he tightened his grip and dug uneven trenches in the ground. He tried to scream. Fear stole his voice and was taking the last of his breath. He surrendered to the fall.

Sean coughed and sucked on the air as he landed on the bed. He took in another deep lungful of air. Fear and anxiety replaced the pleasure of finding himself in his bed. He took in a deep lungful of air hoping to ease the pain which bloomed in his chest. It wasn't pain. It was pleasure. An orgasm quivered in his groin. His cock hard, wet, needy. It bounced up in down in the air as if someone or something stroking him, pumping him, priming him. A deep guttural moan escaped his throat. He ejaculated. Cum, thick and hot spewed from his cock. He smiled from the rush as he felt the warmth of his orgasm splash over his chest and stomach, mixing with his sweat and body hair. His body quivered and shook as the spasm died. The pleasure was replaced by anxiety and fear. He realized something in the fall was different. For the first time, he hadn't been alone. There was someone in the fall with him. A block of ice settled into his tailbone and made his body shiver. The mattress shifted. A warm billow of air rose around him. Terror wrapped its fingers around Sean's throat. He tried to swallow the lump.

"Morning, honey," Neal whispered. He snuggled up against Sean's back. Neal's hands caressed his body, running his fingers up his chest, his neck, then across Sean's lips. Sean sucked Neal's fingers into his mouth. Layers of charred skin peeled away against the edge of his teeth. He opened his eyes to the blistered and bloody fingers pulling out of his mouth.

"Miss me?" Neal spoke through bruised and swollen lips. He grinned, exposing a mouthful of charred, blackened teeth. His lower lip split open. Blood oozed. His naked body blistered and smoldered singed the sheets. Plumes of smoke drifted off the bed. The scent of burnt flesh ripened the air. "I'll never leave you, Sean,"

The fear that had silenced Sean relented. He screamed, tumbled out of bed, and hit the floor hard. A sharp pain exploded from his tailbone shattering the lump of ice. Despite the nauseating ache, he pulled himself up and looked across the bed. It was empty. He pulled back the sheets and patted the mattress. Stray body hair scattered across the sheet. There was no way in or out. He wanted to believe it was nothing more than a dream. *A manifestation of your mind.* That wouldn't explain the haunting memories of Neal, which saturated the fabric.

Sean stood with the aid of the bedframe and waited for the strength in his legs to return. In the bathroom, Sean looked into the mirror while the water ran warm. He didn't recognize the man staring back at him. Rough morning whiskers, hollow eyes which appeared empty - lifeless. He leaned over the sink and splashed water on his face then looked back at the mirror. Water dripped from his jaw and chin, fell to his chest and became lost in the tangle of hair. "It was a dream, nothing more," Sean reassured himself. *Are you sure?* The man in the mirror said. Sean shut off the light and walked out of the bathroom ignoring the stranger's comment.

The bed called to him. He paused in the middle of the bedroom. The energy drained from his body as if someone had pulled a plug in the bottom of his feet. He wanted nothing more than to crawl across the mattress and collapse. He took a step closer to the foot of the bed. The clock struck eleven. The chime ripped through the silence. The blood in his veins ran cold. He followed the echo into the living room as the last of the eleven faded away. Another moment lost to time.

He poured a scotch and took a swig of the warm liquid. Savoring the burn, he refilled his glass. A bluish glow filled the room and caught Sean's attention. He walked over to the coffee table. His phone had awoken as well. He stared at the blue background wondering what triggered the phone, then remembered the messages hidden within. His fingers trembled as he reached for the phone. It felt cold in his hand.

His husband's name appeared at the top—the last message he ever recorded. Sean tried to find comfort in the memories of their nightly phone calls when Neal was ready to leave work. Most nights Sean picked up the phone, anxious to hear his husband's voice. *Why didn't I pick up that night? Did I ever not take his call?* His mind questioned. His thumb hovered over the delete button. Instead, he pushed play and lifted the phone to his ear.

"Hi, honey. Sorry, I'm running a bit late." Neal's deep voice filled with love tore at Sean's heart. "Problems with a patient. I'm leaving now, so I'll see you in about an hour depending on traffic. I love you, Bye." His voice died and left Sean feeling cold as if he were the one six-feet in the ground.

A numbness surrounded Sean as Neal's voice lingered in the room with him. He felt neither here nor there. Someplace else. Looking in on someone else's life. Always on the outside. Memories of his former life remained hidden in the dark corners of the room—and his mind. Ghosts of lost time. They drew the air from the room. Death by asphyxiation. They whispered words, and talked of things he didn't, or couldn't remember. Exhausted, Sean left the ghosts to their mumbling and walked into the bedroom. He popped two sleeping pills with the last of his drink and looked around the room.

Photographs of their life together lined the walls and bookcases. They were no longer a comfort to Sean. The eyes in the images mocked him, teased him, tormented him. He felt exposed and naked against the stares. He looked at the bed wanting nothing more than to crawl into it and pull the covers over his body. He tossed the sheets back. Grass, mud, and moss-covered the foot of the bed. Memories of the last fall drifted back into his mind. Ghosts floating through space. Sean looked at his feet. There were ill-manicured but clean. *The fall was real.* "No, it's a manifestation of..." Sean couldn't remember the rest, or where he had heard it from. The thought gasped and died.

Unable to sleep in the bed, Sean walked back into the living room. Ignoring the ghosts, he fell onto the couch and succumbed to sleep.

Sean awoke to blinding sunlight coupled with the pain of a pill and alcohol-induced hangover. He covered his eyes with his arm to block out the worst of the morning sun. The scent of his night sweat laced with scotch hovered over the couch and stung his nose. With his cock stiff and wet against his belly, he ran his hand down his skin, feeling the dampness of his body's heat cling to the hair covering his body. He followed the tuft of hair just below the navel. His cock and pubic hair were wet from arousal. He pulled on his cock desperate for a moment of release. He moaned, hoping the sound of pleasure might bring him closer, but his tormented mind wouldn't give in to his efforts. His cock softened in his grip. The room spun over and upside down as he pushed himself to a sitting position. Elbows on knees, he palmed the sleep from his eyes.

One leg felt shorter than the other as one foot slumbered. He limped through the bedroom in a dazed mental state. Half asleep. Half drunk. He managed to find his way into the bathroom. He turned on the water, removed his boxers, and stepped into the shower without waiting for the water to warm. The icy water cascaded over his body. He shivered as the chill engulfed him, then crystalized and shattered the fog in his mind.

The shower door rattled. Sean held his breath as he felt a presence enter the shower with him. He gasped as a finger ran down the length of his spine.

"Morning honey," Neal whispered. His warm breath kissed the back of Sean's neck. His husband's fingers crawled downward following the crack of his ass.

"Oh, God." Sean moaned. Despite the paralyzing fear he bent his knees and allowed Neal's hand to move between his legs.

"You didn't wait for me." Neal kissed Sean's neck then turned him around.

"Neal?" Sean looked into the handsome face of his husband. The dark growth of morning whiskers covered his lips, chin, and jaw. His black hair dripped with water. "It's not, possible."

"What's wrong, honey. You look like you've seen a ghost." He laughed and pulled Sean into his arms.

The tight, coarse hair on Neal's chest tickled Sean's nose. He inhaled the warm, musky scent of Neal's body, the same smell he woke to for over a year. Sean listened to the soft, gentle beat of Neal's heart and nestled his face against the warmth of his skin. He looked into Neal's dark green eyes, "I...I thought you were dead."

"Dead," he chuckled. "Sweetheart, it must have been a bad dream, does this feel like I'm dead?" He took Sean's hand and placed it between them. Neal's cock was erect, warm, and wet with need. Sean palmed it making Neal moan. His breath was sweet and warm against Sean's face. " I've missed you, so much. Make love to me," Neal whispered. He smiled and turned Sean around. He ran his cock up and down the crack of Sean's ass.

"Oh, God." Sean gasped as Neal entered him and forced their body against the shower wall.

"Forever, my love." Neal bit Sean's neck and ran his fingers over Sean's chest, pinching and tugging on Sean's nipples before running his hand up Sean's neck and over his face. "I'll never leave you, babe," Neal whispered.

Forever. The word haunted Sean's mind as he sucked Neal's fingers into his mouth matching the thrusts of Neal's hips. Memories flashed in Sean's mind like a distorted silent movie. He watched the flicker of movement as a mahogany coffin is lowered into an open grave. He looked around the cemetery. The grieving black and white faces of friends and family stare at him in contempt and guilt. He backed away from their silent screams as Neal came walking through the crowd. Flames burst from the ground and licked his naked skin. Small fissures erupted across Neal's body. The skin blackened and peeled away as the flames ate at him.

The air in the bathroom became laden with the heat of the flames. Sean struggled for breath. The temperature in the room continued to rise. He turned around. He was alone. He opened the shower door and peered out into the bathroom. He couldn't see anyone through the stream.

Sean leaned against the shower wall and wept. His eyes focused on the drain as the water vortexed into it. The drain seemed to shift. It spread and grew larger the longer he looked at it. The drain opened and closed like the mouth of a fish. Razor-sharp teeth spun and gnawed, eating away at the fiberglass. Sean grabbed onto the frame of the shower door as the tub disappeared. His feet dangled above the void. Flames rose from the darkness, licking and biting the soles of his feet. His grip weakened. The metal frame tore into the flesh of his fingers. He could no longer hold himself. His fingers slipped off the railing one by one. He began to fall.

Darkness surrounded Sean. A cold chill swept across his dampened body. The night was too thick to see. He blinked and waited for his eyes to adjust. The moon, as if answering his prayer for sight, appeared through the clouds. It's light dotting the landscape with a pearlescent white glow.

The graveyard came alive with the touch of the moon. Tombstones, shimmering in the light, cast gray shadows across the muted green grass. An owl called out. Another one answered. Wings fluttered. The wind moaned.

In the distance, a woman stood near a grave. Sean walked toward her. She ignored his approach. The woman looked familiar, but Sean couldn't place her. The wind made her auburn hair billow around her face, and toy with the bottom seam of her trench coat.

The cold, softness of the soil sank between Sean's toes. He looked down and noticed for the first time that he was naked and aroused. He covered himself as best he could with his hands then glanced at the headstone. They were standing over his husband's grave.

"Don't I know you?" he asked. The woman didn't respond. She remained with her head down looking at the grave. "Why are you here? Did you know my husband?" She raised her head. Her movement slow, purposeful. Her hair cascaded across her face. With a knowing smile, she looked at him.

"You're confused," she said. "Or sick. Perhaps both. Neal thought it was the latter."

"You knew my husband?"

"Neal was my husband. Not yours." Her smile faltered.

"Why are you lying to me? Who are you?"

"I told you, I'm Mrs. Parker. Marlena Parker."

A memory flashed through Sean's head, but it was too fast

and blurred to see it with any clarity. "You must be mistaken. Neal and I've been married for..." he stopped to think. *How long were we married?*

"You can't remember, can you?"

"But I have his ring." He reached out his hand to show the woman. His finger was bare. "I must have lost it. No, it's the last thing I have to remember him by." Sean fell to his knees and patted the damp grass in search of the wedding band.

"You won't find it."

"What have you done with it?" Sean looked up at the woman who called herself Mrs. Parker.

"You won't find one, because there never was one. You were never married to Neal."

"Why do you keep saying that?"

"You have an attachment disorder. You find someone who seems to care for you, and you become obsessed with them. My husband, Neal was your psychotherapist. He was trying to help you overcome your obsessions."

"No..." Sean wanted to say more but an intense wave of emotions knocked the breath out of him. "Please..." He gasped and looked up at her. "We loved each other."

"Loved? You're not capable of that emotion. He was nothing more than an obsession for you. An obsession that killed him."

"What? No, don't say...oh my God, no." Sean suddenly realized where he knew the woman from. He dug his fingers into the earth of the grave. "I met you in Neal's office." The memories came flooding back.

"Remember what we talked about, Sean." Neal continued. "These emotional attachments you have are a manifestation of your mind. You create elaborate scenarios in your mind, then act them out if they were real. You're only hurting yourself, Sean. Your obsessions scare people..." A buzzer crackled through the air.

"Mr. Parker, your wife is here."

"Thank you, Melissa."

Sean's neck and face burned with anger. *He's been cheating on me. No, it's not possible. He loves me. We love each other.* Sean stood.

"Is something wrong, Sean?"

"No." He said but couldn't look at the man he loved. He didn't want to see the lies in Neal's face. Sean grabbed his coat and opened the door. A woman stood as Sean entered the waiting room. Her auburn hair fell over her shoulders and caressed her breasts. Fire engine red lipstick accentuated her lips. Sean imagined Neal, his Neal, lying naked with this woman as she smeared his lips, cheeks, and neck with that slutty color.

"Hi." The woman smiled, then passed Sean and walked into Neal's arms. They kissed and walked into the office.

Sean wanted to say something. No, that wasn't right. He wanted to hurt her. He wanted to gouge her eyes out and shove them down her throat. Neal was his and no one else's. As he turned to leave and noticed the woman's purse sitting on the chair. He looked around to make sure he was alone, then grabbed the woman's phone and ran out of the room.

Sean collapsed on the ground. The cold, grave dirt stuck to his tear and sweat-dampened face. He lifted his head and look at the woman standing over him. "This has to be a dream. Please, tell me it's a dream." He laughed and rolled over on his back and stared at the star-filled night as the memories continue to bombard his splintered mind.

Sean sat in his car. White knuckles gripped the steering wheel. Neal hadn't been home for two days. Tears welled in his eyes as he watched Neal come out of the office alone.

"Neal," Sean yelled. He stepped out of the car.

"Sean, what are you doing here?"

"Please, don't leave me. I don't care what you've done in the past. I forgive you. Babe, please come home."

"Sean, you need to get back in your car and go home. You're confused. We can't do this here. I'm late for..."

"For her."

"Sean, she's my wife." He gave Sean a disappointed look. "You're not taking the medication I prescribed, are you?"

"I love you, Neal." Sean opened his arms for a hug. Neal held out his hand to keep a distance between them.

"Sean, promise me you'll go home and take your medicine, or I'm calling the police and having you taken in for the night."

"Why are you doing this?"

"Good-night, Sean." Neal clicked the remote, opened the door, then closed it and drove off without even looking back.

Sean walked to his car as the man he loved pulled away. "I can't let you go like this," Sean muttered. "I have to make you understand." He tried to hold onto the love. The only thing Sean felt was rage.

"No, please, no. It's not true." Sean got to his hands and knees determined to fight the lies this woman put into his head. He pounded his fists against Neal's grave. Sean's body became a raging inferno. Sweat poured down his face. His stomach clenched. He heaved spitting what little was in his stomach. His hands sank into the soil. The world blurred and shifted. He began to fall.

That night Neal called his wife to let her know he was running late, Sean sat in his car and listened to the love in Neal's voice for the woman. He waited twenty, thirty, then forty minutes. Sean remembered feeling numb as drove his car and parked it lengthwise across the road. There was no anger, no fear. He knew what he had to do. In the final moments, he let go and said a quiet good-bye to his husband, the only man he ever loved. Sean, with the windows down in his car, heard the familiar clanking of Neal's engine coming around the bend in the road. The headlights glared at Sean. The excitement was too much for Sean to handle. He ejaculated in his pants as the smell of rubber against asphalt rose through the air. Neal's car turned to avoid hitting Sean. Neal lost control and went over the edge of the cliff. Sean got out of his car and watched as Neal's car nosedive into the valley, then explode in a fireball of flames and smoke.

Sean fell to his knees and cried at the loss of his husband. "I'm so sorry, Neal." He looked out into the darkness. The cold winter wind bit his tear-streaked face. He turned and saw his car sitting there, still running, still waiting. He stood and walked toward the car. He got in, placed the car in drive. He hit the accelerator and screamed as he drove the car over the cliff.

He felt the weightlessness as the car seemed to hang in the air, dangling over life and death, moving without motion, slow, lifeless, formless. A memory of Neal and him going over the top of a rollercoaster blinked in his mind as the car began to descend. His stomach rose in his throat. The thrill of the fall then Neal appeared in the passenger seat. His burnt and bloody face turned and smiled at Sean.

"You said you wanted forever, and forever you shall have."

"Do you believe me now?" The woman asked. She was motionless except for the wind. Her cold, expressionless face stared down at him.

"Make it stop, please."

"Stop?" She laughed. "You must be joking. You murdered my husband. You destroyed our lives."

"If what you say is true why not have me arrested?" Sean tried to reason even though he knew the truth within the memories.

"That would have been too easy. You wouldn't have suffered enough. Neal and I decided to make our own punishment. This is all that's left, Mr. Wick. You'll never have a moment of peace from this point forward." The woman turned and walked away.

"Wait, please, what do you mean?" Sean cried. He sucked in a painful lung of air. His hands sank farther into the grave. He tried to knead his hands out of the ground, but something held him down.

A tremor rumbled through the cemetery. The epicenter Neal's grave. The ground caved in pulling Sean deeper into the ground. Sean screamed as two charred hands reached out of the smoldering earth and grabbed his head. He felt the radiant heat of the burning flames of hell against his skin. He sank farther into the ground, getting closer to Neal's body, which lay somewhere beneath him. And then he fell.

Sean's body slammed against the fiberglass tub. His head smacked against the ridge jolting him awake. The hot water cascaded over him and stung his heat reddened skin. He looked around in a steamy daze unsure of where he was. He pulled himself up on his hands and knees and turned off the water. With trembling legs, he stood and opened the shower door.

Sean stood in the bathroom doorway. The steam from the shower engulfed him as rivulets of water trickled down his back and chest. A puddle of cooling water gathered at his feet while he waited, unable to step into the bedroom. Ghosts lingered in the darkness, and he had many of them. *Acceptance is the first step in recovery.* A voice, not quite unknown to him, echoed in his mind. He now kept the light on a timer, so it always came on as the light of the day died. An icy finger brushed across the nap of his neck. A breath caught in his throat. The light timer clicked illuminating the bedroom in a soft, white glow.

THE GAY AGENDA
JAKE NEVILLE

Pink light spewing from the mouth of a slutty Luna Park man painted across the length of a renovated Victorian terrace? I mean, it doesn't *not* sound like the place. This *is* Fitzroy. And I *am* at the destination pin. Empusa? Name matches. Let me just check her message. Hey J, yep, yep, yep, meet at Empusa... Fitzroy...back lounge better than main bit...yep, it all looks right.

Fuck, it's cold. Why do we wear jackets in the day, but as soon as we're going out it's like, nah you're a fuckwit for dressing for the right weather conditions. Wish I'd worn my Tigers jersey at least, goosebumps now. Oh my God, I look like such a freak just standing here. The bouncer is just staring at me. Is he biting his lip? Whatever, good thing there's no line. Better be worth ditching the boys.

License out. Smile. Yes, it's gold. Yes, it's Queensland. Yes, I do miss the weather. Wallet in pocket. Those eyes. How did they get the Luna Park eyes to swing back and forth like that, while staying trained on you? The mouth is huge - they must have carved into the wall! That pink is blinding. It does look sick on my skin though. I look like Barney. Some stairs. Oh, I get it. It's covered in velvet because it's the tongue. Clever.

Thudding isn't so distant anymore. It's getting clearer. It's familiar. It's poppy. It's Kylie. Kylie Minogue, I mean. Don't know the song though. Mum loves her. Only reason I can pick that one. Shit, did I miss the pay station? Fuck it, mustn't have been one. Won't be long here anyway.

Reminds me. "hey just got in, want a drink?" "daddy's paying ;)".

Cunt, it is *sprawling* down here. How is there still one more flight of stairs before I even get down to the dancefloor? I can see everyone from up here. Wonder if I can see Jess at all. There are so many people. Heaps dancing, a bunch at the bar. Colorful too. A bit livelier than some other clubs I've toured. Wait, no. She said she's in the back lounge. Won't be able to spot her, dingus. Fuck, she's making me work for it. Keep heading down. Woah! Almost went arse over. Can't believe how many feathers there are. Someone should probably give these steps a sweep.

Most haven't noticed my arrival. Although, there are a pack of lads nearby who haven't taken their eye off me. Are they judging me? Wanting to square up? Or...No, I'll just, um, head to the bar. Go get that drink. Excuse me, sorry. Not moving? Whatever, duck under. The bird should do it. Push. Made it. Wait, what did she want?

No reply yet.

Uh, what do girls drink? Cider? I'll just lean my head over, surely I'll be noticed soon. Can't even see the tender over this chick next to me. Are you even ordering? She's got massive hair. Fuck, it goes all the way down to her ass that's sticking out the bottom of her shorts. And, fishnets. She isn't here to fuck spiders.

"Yeah, can I just-" She just turned around. She's staring right at me. "Get a cider and-"

"Make it two," she says. Real breathy, and low.

"Oh, it's not for me, it's-" Hard to talk over the music.

"What's your name?" Her smile is infectious. Small tits though. But, tight waist.

"Huh?"

"I said, do you wanna dance?"

Oh my God.

"Yes."

Take her hand. She's flipping her blonde hair and dancing me through the crowd. They're moving for us, I think. I'll get those drinks later. New song coming on. Do I know this one? Hope so, otherwise I'll look like a tool. Fuck, it's just some EDM. Cool sound though. Spacey. Fast. God, she's not pulling any punches. Hand on my thigh, hips swinging, hair tossing. Did she just run her hand over her vag? I'm just here bopping. Uh, try something. A spin? What is this? The 70s? She's laughing. That's good at least.

Strobes now. Darkness between flashes of blue light. Looks like stop motion. She's getting something out from her bra. A bottle. Small. Holding it to her nose. Deep breath. Putting it up to my nose now. She's blocked a nostril. Yeah, um, I guess? It's chemically. She's pulled it away and—woah...

Is it just me, or am I really fucking good at dancing? Spin *her* around this time. Doof, doof, doof, doof. She's bending over, run your hands down those fishnets. She's coming back up, shaking that ass. Don't even see the jiggle, just flashes of it from side to side. She throws a smile over the shoulder. Doof, doof, doof, doof.

Strobes off, pink spotlights cut through the blue. Her motions are fluid now. Wait, Jess! Uh, I should probably find her first.

"I've gotta go for a sec."

She's grabbed my hand.

"Plenty more where that came from," she whispers in my ear. Did I hear that right? She winks. Huh, kinda heavy on the makeup now that I think about it. She's back to dancing. Is she dancing away from me?

Grab her hand.

"Where?"

She smirks. Too good of an opportunity to pass up. Who doesn't want free blow? Maybe if I play my cards right...

She's dancing backward through the crowd, beckoning. Oh, God. This is too good to be true. There's so many people here. Uh, I'm losing her. Lucky I can see her hair over the tops of everyone. Duck and weave. Slide through.

Couple of shirtless guys. I hate when they take their shirts off, yeah I get you're more ripped than I'll ever be. A couple of them are wearing chains? What the fuck, are they fags? They're intense at least. Whatever, it's twenty-nineteen, you can handle them.

"Excuse me."

Staring me down. Fine then, I'll just walk in between you.

He's grabbed me! One of them have me! Wrapped in his arms! Hairy arms. Strong. Got to get away. Can't lose her.

"I want to eat your face!" He shouts in my ear. Get off! Shake free. Spin around.

"Go fuck yourself!" Voice cracked at the end of that. Didn't think they'd be so...They're not doing anything. Just standing there. Still. Not dancing, just staring. One of them sips from a...goblet? Looks like wine. Jesus Christ, I'm covered in glitter.

"He's mine," she says, jumping in between us. Thank God, because I would have decked them so hard. She's got my wrist, dragging me away. Quick, turn around and flip them off. Swear they weren't wearing contacts before. Orange eyes. Slits. Like snakes. They know it's not Halloween right?

Ouch! Your nails are digging into me! She hasn't noticed, still dragging me through the crowd. Fucking stop! Rip her hand from mine. There's blood there! She's turned around. Shouldn't have done that, she looks pissed. For a second. She's seen the blood. Super sorry now. Mood swings. Keep that in mind.

Kiss it better? Sure. I love when chicks do that puppy dog face. That actually does feel better. Back to dancing now, huh? Alright, I can dig. Not usually a fan of club music, but this is dope. Punch the air. Hey, my forearm's not bleeding anymore. She's dancing toward a door. Is that where Jess is?

Wait, shit. Did she reply to me? "yes pls daddy", "heading for a dart". Where is she going for the dart? Can't see her. Can't see the entrance. So many people

She's pushing the door open now. She's bathed in orange light. Smoke's just falling out from that room. Disappearing all over the blue dance floor. Is that the smokers? Must be where Jess is. Or is Jess out front?

Fuck it. Let's go. This chick's fangin' for it.

Isn't it usually ladies first? Whatever, I'll go then.

More stairs? Did they drill a coal mine into this place too? They spiral downward. Clanging footsteps. Little echo. Heavy door thud. Club sounds distant now. Thick walls. Her footsteps are behind me. Loud echo now. Can barely see through all this smoke. Or breathe for that matter. Barely hear the club now. But, there's another sound. Coming from below. Crunchy. Kinda old. From a gramophone. Closer now. Sounds like a chick singing. Some kind of 50s song or something. Weird. Haven't heard that music anywhere but Nan's.

A groan. Was that just a groan I heard? From below? Turn to see if she heard it. She's just smiling at me. Smile back. Don't seem like a loser. Just keep heading down. Almost there. The song's getting clearer. Can't hear the club.

Stairs open up into a long corridor. Kinda like those French catacombs I saw in Europe. Didn't even know Melbourne had these running under it. Seems to stretch on forever. Crackling. Are they allowed to light lanterns down here? Would explain the smoke. There's that song. It's so undiluted here.

I wanna be loved by you, just you. Breathy singer. Definitely ancient sound.

And nobody else but you. Those moans! Sound like they're right next to me!

I wanna be loved by you alooone. For fuck's sake, if this is a swingers...

"Boop-boop-de-boop!" She whispers in time, winking at me. Look, let's just get the shit and go. You've come this far. Then you can meet up with Jess and the boys, and still have a ripper night.

Me? Lead? Again? But, I don't know-

"Which way?"

Pointing to the left. Okay. Man, when was this place built? Walls look like sandstone. Ground is cobblestone. Coming lose. Better watch my step. I can hear panting. Not too far along. Looks like...a prison cell up ahead. Iron bars. Rusty. Panting coming closer. So is the cell. Quieten the footsteps. Don't want any unnecessary attention.

There's a cot in the cell. And there's two dudes fucking on top of it! They're puffing like dogs. Eyes away.

"Give me that seed. Give me it. I want your gift. So bad," one of them says. Pretend like everything's fine. Keep calm. What the fuck is this pla-

Ow! Rolled ankle. Fucking cobblestone. Who the fuck invented cobblestone! Who the fuck though it was a good idea to make a path with cracks all through it! Slowly get up. Can't put too much pressure on it. Just breathe it out. So embarrassing. Did she see? Turn around. But cool.

She's just smiling. That's it. Not even going to help? Bitch.

"Much farther?"

Cold! So cold! Who just shoves a hand down someone's pants uninvited! Jumped so far forward. She must think I'm a lunatic. Can still feel her freezing handprint on my ass. She's giggling. It echoes. I really don't want to be here anymore.

"On your left." She breathes.

On the left is a door. Big. Wooden. Is Frankenstein locked up back there?

Push it open. Loud splintering creak. The noise! How did I not hear it before!

The grunts. The squeals. The chatter. The slurping. The laughter.

Door's swung all the way open.

There I am.

There they are. Looking at me.

Dudes shackled to walls, being fucked in the arse. Being fucked in the mouth. Dudes in chains. Dudes in leather. Dudes drinking wine from goblets. Dudes dressed in feathers. Dudes dressed in sequins. Dudes in nothing at all. Dudes everywhere.

No one's moving. No one's making a sound. No sound at all. Apart from the crackling fire, and that crunchy gramophone. That fucking song!

Boop-boop-de-boop!

Can't back out now. Just walk through. Smile, I guess. All you can hear is my shoes.

Did someone just snarl at me? Who did that?

They're growling now. Low. Where is it coming from? To the side, further down.

It's coming from a bald chick. Tall. Wait, no. That's not a chick. It's a *guy*! In makeup! And chick's clothes! With a hairnet on!

Wait a minute.

Oh, God.

Oh, no.

No.

This can't be real.

Just turn around.

I know you don't want to.

But you have to.

Slowly.

There.

I knew it. Fuck, I knew it. She doesn't have her hair on! *He* doesn't have *his* hair on!

Face forward.

Keep walking. He's right behind you. Grinning.

What am I going to do?

There has to be a way out.

Keep calm.

There has to.

End of the room.

Another big wooden door.

Reckon you could smash it open if you just...

Run! Run! Fast as you can! Keep going! Why can't my legs carry me as fast as my body wants to! Please don't slip! Fly! Fucking go! You're doing it! Just keep runni-

Pain all through my shoulder. Flaring. Door swung open. Wood crashing against stone. Falling forward. Onto my face. Onto sand. Splutter. Spit. Got to get up. Got to keep moving. Where are you? What is this room? Look up, open your eyes.

It's a cistern. Massive. An island of sand in the middle. Two huge wooden beams making an X in the centre of it. And, blood. Pouring. Like waterfalls from the roof and into a river. It's running around the island. Like a...moat. Nowhere else to go. Got to go back. Spin around. Oh fuck, they're coming. All of them. And she's leading them. I mean, he's leading them. The gramophone's stopped.

Loud, piercing shrieks and growls. Can hear flesh and bone ripping, snapping. They're transforming. Into monsters. Claws growing from hands, teeth growing in mouths, backs hunching, spines protruding, skin greying, and hair sprouting, horns erupting. Wings, like a bat's, shooting from his body. His fishnets rip, and there's fangs! Fangs coming out of that sparkling red lipped mouth!

Don't be scared, I've done this before. They start chanting together. Coming closer.

Show me your teeth. A gust of wind. Freezing. His wings are arched, and they're flapping. He's coming in fast. Hand outstretched!

Feel it gripped around my collar. Nails digging into my neck. Moving fast. Backward. Feet off the floor. Air flying past. Closed eyes.

Motherfucker! Spasms all through my back, whiplashed neck, piercing headache. Splinters all through my shirt. Not moving anymore. Can barely breathe. Feet still off the floor. Cold hand still got me...

Open eyes. His head is pressing toward mine. Foul breath. Can see the rest of them approaching, galloping, running, scuttling. Can't hear them. Ears ringing. He blinks, with a second set of eyelids. They're...orange too. With slits. Like a snake's. Tongue sliding out of that gaunt, made up, skull. It's forked. It's travelling across my jaw. Wet. Tasting my ear. Scaly. Moving to my mouth. Caressing my lips.

Show me your teeth. Hearing's coming back.

Won't let you in. Don't let him in. His nails are digging further...harder...

"CUN-" It's in. Slipped in. Feel it in the back of my throat. Feel it feeling around.

No! They've got my arms! Let me go! Please...

I'm going to love you with your hands tied. They're possessed. Rope burning across wrists. They're outstretched.

Chains freezing across ankles. They've spread them apart. I'm trapped. Strung up.

He's still inside me. Moving deeper. Slowly. Gagging. I'm going to throw up if you go any further. No more, please. Can feel it in my neck...Wretching.

Show me your teeth.

Pulls out. Air is cold. There's so much of it to breathe. Spit all the phlegm out. He's let go of my neck too. Blood's trickling out.

He's on my neck now. Sucking. Getting light headed. Dizzy...Some smaller, lizard looking men are crawling up along my legs. They're slimy. They're coming up along my chest. They're at my neck too. Drinking...

Light's fading...

Got my addictions. Gurgled chanting in my ear...

Can't hold on...They've pulled away...

Stay awake...Keep your eyes open...

Tell me something that'll save me. Chanting is further away. Not too much further.

They're all standing in the moat, cutting their hands open.

Tell me something that'll change me.

Their blood is running into the river, it's sparkling.

He's risen from the moat. The rest hold hands.

Follow him.

Where is he going?

Don't lose sight.

He's flying to the roof of the cistern.

Suctioned to the ceiling like a fly. Scampering about. Looking for something.

A lever.

Pulls it.

Deep, stony rumbling.

Can hear water running.

Sloshing.

Droplets falling onto me.

Plip. Plop.

More droplets.

Rocky tremoring. Something's moving above.

Droplets are a drizzle now.

Smells sweet. Metallic.

Can't lift my head to see.

Drizzle is a heavy stream.

I'm covered.
Look down.
What are you covered in?
It's red.
It's blood.
Blood.
Blood streaming over me.
Sparkling red blood.
Glittering red blood.
Stone pulling away.
Heavy downpour.
Cascade of blood now.
Deafening roar of liquid.
Can't open...eyes.
Can't br...
Need...
Ai...

Is it just me, or am I really fucking good at dancing. Vogue these bitches down. Doof, doof, doof, doof. You ain't shit hunty, drop into the splits. Come back up, shake your ass. Don't even see the queens, just the tops over in the corner. Throw a smile over your shoulder at them. Doof, doof, doof, doof.

Grabbing your cock, hey? Guess you really are keen. *In Your Eyes* is as good a track as any to hook up to. Swing those hips toward him. Hope he likes my jockstrap. It's new. Limited edition glitter waistband. Glowing right now in this blacklight.

Yes, thank you. I would love a sip.

Sweet. Metallic. Rejuvenating.

Grind on him. Show your appreciation.

Doof, doof, doof, doof.

In the distance, can hear something.

Footsteps. Down the stairs.

A boy.

Handsome.

In a hoodie.

Impressionable.

Lost.

Gullible.

Turn back to the stud. He's seen the boy too. His eyes are glowing too. Orange. With slits. Like a snake's.

Come to think of it, so is everyone's.

The hive will eat well tonight, I think.

LAND LINE
MIKE BENDZELA

Phone is in mid-ring as I walk through the door. I'm thinking, Shit—I wonder how long this sucker's been at it. Rick collects old land line telephones, has several throughout the house, the jet-black kind, with curly cords and big, honking receivers. The bells jangle like crazy. I'm sure I won't catch it on time.

I put down my lunch cooler but do not have time to get out of my filthy monkey suit. I trot across the clean kitchen floor in my work boots, snatch the receiver off the hook, say, Hello? but, as I have come to expect, there is just a moment of live, empty air, then a *click*.

I hate missing a phone call. Every time, when I'm racing to catch the phone, I think, *Oh, this is the call I have been waiting for, the most important phone call of my life.*

I hang up and go down to the cellar to wash up and change into my regular clothes, bugged the whole time.

If the caller knew me, then they had to have known I would just be getting in from work, and they would call back if it was important. If they didn't know me...Well, then, maybe it was for Rick. But if it was for Rick, then why call at six when they know he won't be home for another hour? Maybe they don't know either of us. They will probably call back. Or will they? Six-thirty, and no call back. Who could it be? This is the third time. I am bugged by it.

Phone didn't ring again until two days later, a Thursday, just as Rick and I are sitting down for a dinner of tossed salad, chicken parmesan on rice, my favorite simple dish.

I put down my fork. Who could that be? I said, having eaten only the first bite of my chicken. Not that I was annoyed, just surprised. We lead a pretty sedate, workaday life, so it's not unusual for Rick's big black phone to sit quietly for days on end, no messages for us on the machine when we get home, either.

"I don't know," Rick said. "Why don't you pick it up and find out?"

Fine. He's always cranky when he gets home from work. He's a group home administrator. I'm a carpenter, strange mix. He sits inside all day in a shirt and tie and bitches at people, while I'm outside in my monkey suit, swinging from rafters, pounding nails. Getting fucking cold out, too. Rick's reluctant to answer the phone after work because he's in the psychiatric field and he's afraid it might be someone from a group home calling about another disaster. Me, the only calls I get are from family and friends.

"Hello?"

There's that audible air again, the open line fizzing like soda pop, and I start to put the receiver down—only, this time there's no dial tone, so again I say, "Hello?"

"Hello?" a male voice says. I recognize an uncertainty at the other end, who knows where he is.

"Yes, hello."

"Is this Tom, or Rick?"

"This is Tom."

Silence. I sense a tug of approval, like a nibble on a fishing line.

"Are you by yourself, by any chance?"

"You mean, is Rick here?"

Rick is wiping his napkin across his frown, getting ready to take the call.

"No. I'm saying, are you <u>alone</u>."

"No, Rick's here with me."

Click.

That Saturday, Rick and I have our weekly sex. We had spent the day painting the back-porch floor before it got too cold out. We chose to spatter it, maroon background with cream-and-teal speckling. I hadn't seen Rick in casual clothes in a long time. The seat of his jeans was torn twice horizontally, once under each back pocket, so when he bent over his Jockey shorts grinned at me, twice, through the slots. It looked oddly out-of-place on him, not really erotic. Had he been the boy of my dreams, it would have been a completely different story, I might have felt a little faint. Rick is just some forty-one-year-old administrator trying to look funky in street clothes, with his department store undies showing through.

I was cream because Rick had already chosen teal. We dipped our brushes in the paint cans and dribbled our way back towards the exterior door, flinging paint with flicks of our wrists, the fun part. We worked side-by-side, backing up, until we were on the threshold. We stood with heads cocked, trying to decide whether we liked it or not. I shoved my creamy paint brush into the crotch of his jeans.

"The fuck you do that for?"

"Hey, old man. Your skivvies are showing through."

He bent over—he now had a cream-colored crack, like he had sat on a vanilla ice cream cone.

"Well, screw you, buddy." He flicked his brush at me. I could feel dots hitting my face and hair.

That night, sprawled on his belly, he feigned sleep. With legs spread, head turned to one side, smile shaping his face, he looked as though he were having a pleasant dream. I greased myself up with a fistful of "personal lubricant for general use."

"Honey?" he said.

"What is it, darling?"

"I have something to tell you..." Silence. "I'm bisexual."

I yelped. "Yeah, you like men and boys. Let's see what I can do about your little problem."

I try to be gentle, but I'm excited. He tenses up, so I lie full against him, belly to back. I move carefully, working my arms underneath his naked body, squeezing his erection between the mattress and his belly. I nuzzle into the side of his face. He is quiet.

I begin replaying in my head my fantasy about my secret blond friend. I'm riding him the way I ride Rick, only this is his first time, and I'm showing him how it is. Rick moans into the pillow, in both pain and gratitude.

I get up on my arms and begin going at it in earnest. I don't do Rick like this often because it takes too much out of him. A patient, generous lover, he is.

I gasp and lie against his back, holding his shoulders tight—the shoulders of my blond stud.

We lay stuck together a long time, getting colder. After a while, Rick speaks.

"So. How was he?"

"Just fine."

I came down with the flu. I thought I was going to die. Fever, chills, cough that wouldn't let up. I had to lie on the sofa propped on pillows because if I laid flat on my back I couldn't breathe. I was up half the night coughing and sweating and trying to position myself right to breathe. Pneumonia crossed my mind, the bad one, though I knew it wasn't possible. I called my doctor in the morning. He said, "No, not pneumonia, just some infection that's going around," and he told me to keep doing what I was doing. I never bothered to tell him I had been having unprotected anal sex with my husband for years, as that might put ideas into his head. I wanted unbiased opinion.

While Rick was at work, I sat bundled up in bed with a huge, scary novel, popping pills and pumping myself full of cold ginger ale and hot tea. Only time I had to get out of bed was to pee. Could hardly believe it when the old land line began ringing. Sales creeps, most likely, or maybe it was Rick to ask how I'm doing. Luckily, the phone was right next to the bed.

"Hello?"

"Tom."

"Yeah."

"It's me."

"Who?"

"The boy of your dreams."

"Ha, ha, Mike. Haven't you heard? I'm a sick man?"

"My name ain't Mike."

"Who is it? Steve?"

"No. You remember me."

"Yeah, right. Who are you?"

"We were on that rollercoaster together, remember? The ride was so intense, upside down and everything."

I sit upright as a wall stud. My whole body is now a listening organ. My fever and chills seem to subside, no coughing, even though my breaths come and go fast. His voice is quiet, measured, sincere. Somebody young.

"We were masturbating together, even with other people on the rollercoaster, remember? They either miraculously didn't see us, or they didn't care."

I begin to smile, a close-mouthed grin, wide and ironical,

the kind of grin that says, *Ha, ha, I'm not even amused.* The kind of grin that is a cover for intense shock, when you want to look cool and only mildly annoyed with what the other person has said. But I'm on the telephone. There is no one but me in the room.

"Who the <u>hell</u> is this? What has Rick been telling you?"

"Just shut up and listen...Either the other riders didn't care, or it was something everyone did in the dreamworld. As the train was jerking us around and flinging us against one another and pitching us down hills that tugged at our stomachs, we grabbed onto each other, not bothered in the slightest by the other people in the cars. And somehow—you know how these dreams are—you leaned over in your seat and began blowing me, at the same time that I leaned over and blew you. Somehow, we were doing each other at the same time in our seats on a rollercoaster. Then we fell down a hill that didn't end—we kept flying down, everyone screaming like it was a plane crash about to happen, the g-force flattening our stomachs, remember? It felt like we were going to have an orgasm. And then, right before you woke up, it felt like you were blowing yourself before the crash came—"

My face flushed with anger, but I couldn't open my mouth to interrupt him. I wanted to see just how much Rick had told the guy, how far he had taken it. He got everything right, the whole dream, right down to little details I didn't know I had told Rick. But it had been morning when I told him about it, I'd just had the dream and was groggy, so maybe Rick remembered more about my dream than I remembered telling him. Whatever, this fucker on the other end of the line, whoever he was, was doing a damn good job telling me my own wet dream. He sounded like he was even getting into it, like he had been there, and while this spooked me (probably because I had been reading that scary novel), I knew that I would have to kill Rick.

Before I could find the right insults to pump into the

telephone, the guy said, "I'll call back later," and hung up, as if someone had come into the room.

The scene was ugly. Rick kept insisting, till his face was shiny red, that he hadn't told anyone about my fucking dream, as he hadn't even remembered me telling him about it. And, for Christ's sake, why the hell would he want to tell somebody else about his husband's wet dream in the first place? It made no goddamn sense because whose fucking business was it?

"That's what I want to know, asshole. That fucker on the phone got it all right, and you're the only one I told it to. Who the hell else am I going to tell something like that to? I've been sick and shut up in this house for a week. I can't believe you'd do something like this while I'm sick."

"Well, you must have told someone else about it, that's all I can say, because I didn't say a fucking word."

"I'm telling you, I told nobody but you. You had to have opened your mouth to some guy, some trick—"

"You're crazy!"

"I'll tell you who's crazy, that little butt buddy of yours who decided in his sick little mind to call me and fuck with my head by telling me my own dream."

"I don't have a <u>butt buddy</u>, and I didn't tell anyone about your goddamn dream."

"Maybe you put him up to it, thought it would be a funny joke. But now you know just how not funny it was—"

"I don't believe this...What's your temperature, anyway?"

"Don't try to blame this on my fever."

I threw the bottle of pills at him, but it missed and cracked up against the wall, tablets everywhere.

He left the room, saying, "Now I know something's wrong with you."

We stopped speaking. Unprecedented in our ten years together. He slept in the guest room. I coughed and sweated all night on the sofa. I hated him for betraying me and embarrassing me and going on like it wasn't his fault. And the gall of trying to tell me I was imagining things or hallucinating! It was like the end of the world. I began to consider when I would move out, where I would go.

He got up for work early and slunk out of the house without even saying goodbye. So, my fault, is it?

"You're a real dumbass for calling here again. Who are you?"

"I already told you. I'm the boy of your dreams."

"You know how much shit you've caused here, you fucker?"

I was speaking as much in reference to Rick as to the guy on the phone.

"If I'm not the boy of your dreams, then how come I know you were sweating all night and tossing and turning and not getting any sleep?"

"Because, asshole, you've been with Rick, and Rick's got a big mouth, and apparently, he doesn't know what a sick fucker you are."

There was a long silence. I got the feeling he was trying to let me come to some sort of realization. I recalled those phone calls a few weeks earlier, when the caller kept hanging up.

"Why have you been calling here? I know you're the one who's been hanging up on me."

"You know more about me than you might think."

"Yeah? Like that you're a sick bastard? You like to harass fags, is that it? You're fucking with the wrong guy."

"Listen. I'm tall, about six-one. I have shoulder-length, ginger blond hair, blue eyes, nice teeth. I'm that youngster you've been banging in your head. And let me tell you something, I'm not sorry in the least for causing the mess between you and Rick. In fact, I'm glad."

"You little son of a bitch."

This was too much. Rick must blab everything, not only my

dreams but my fantasies. Now this fucker was trying to use this to break us up.

"I don't believe I'm hearing this shit."

"Better believe it...Remember last night? We were riding bikes out in the country. There was no sound. No sound at all."

I sat there, holding the big receiver of the telephone up to my head, feeling like one of Rick's mental patients. I suddenly didn't know where I was, I was just testing this receiver against my ear, like a conch shell, listening to the roaring silence.

The guy stayed quiet on the other end, letting me hang there until I could settle down, catch my breath. Then he cleared his throat and spoke in a smooth, quiet voice, calm as a friend after some misunderstanding has been cleared up.

"Yeah. Riding bikes together. Right, Tom?"

Last night, all alone with my fever, I had been lying there on the sofa, shivering but hot, thinking, what the hell? And I reached into my shorts and began to massage myself toward arousal. I dreamed up the biking scenario.

The caller went on, "I was up front, and you pedaled up close behind me to look me up and down."

He begins spelling it all out for me, what I was thinking, feeling. In my fantasy, we're going very fast, pedaling like mad. I'm watching him pump the pedals in front of me, watching his blond hair blowing in the wind, watching his hips shift back and forth as he works the pedals. I can see all the muscles in his bare back. And there's that firm ass encased in black riding shorts. When we get to our destination, I will peel those shorts right off that ass...

"You were thinking what you'd like to do to me as you pedaled up behind me, staring at my ass."

I slam down the receiver. In a beat, the bells of the telephone ring out again. I watch it ring, even though there is nothing to see but a ringing telephone. He couldn't call back that quickly, it has to be somebody else that has been trying to get through, a weird coincidence. I gather myself before I pick up. I'm shaking — is it the fever? If the caller senses my distress, I will say it's due to being sick...

"Hello?"

"Don't ever fucking hang up on me when I'm talking to you."

I slam the phone down again, and it rings. It rings a long time before I can manage to calm down enough to pick it up. I pick up and just lay the receiver on the table. I have to get out of this house. Go somewhere, anywhere.

I can hear his voice, tiny as hell, but clear, yelling up at me from the table:

"Listen fucker. You're gonna hear what I have to say. If not now then tonight. Yeah, tonight, you're gonna hear from me. When you fall asleep, I'll be there."

I pick up the receiver with a tight fist, as though it's a small animal I mean to crush in my hand.

"What the hell do you want from me?"

"That's more like it. Now, the question is not what I want from you, it's what you've been wanting from me. I almost couldn't walk the day after you banged your little husband there...I'm not some crank caller. I'm not some trick your husband picked up. You think about me often enough, you should know. You never leave me alone, so now I'm not gonna leave you alone. You screw me whenever you feel like it, even when your *husband* isn't there to take it like a man. Now it's time for paybacks. You ready to have me come over there and take my pound of flesh?"

All I could say was, "You–"

"Yes, me. It's my turn. I'm coming over soon. Your little blond dream boy is on his way up. But first, that husband of yours–"

This time, he hangs up.

I listen to the dead-line a long time, as if waiting for him to pick up again. I return the receiver to its cradle, gingerly, afraid it might ring out.

My face is on fire, my mouth, lips, tongue, throat all dried out. I lie back and wonder if I really am in too deep a fever. Maybe Rick is right. All those days of relentless hot flashes, night sweats, the thermometer topping out at 105. I've heard of fevers which burn up the brain and cause hallucinations. Oh, how I have been abusing the poor man these last few days! I am sicker than I think and making his life miserable. I should call an ambulance, before it is too late.

No. I am just trying to deny the conversation I just had.

The bells shatter me, like a shotgun blast.

I shout into the receiver, "What do you want now?"

"Tom? Is this Rick's friend, Tom?"

Oh my God. A woman from Rick's group home. I can't get anything to come out of my mouth.

"What is going on there? Did you know that Rick didn't come to work today? Can you hear me? This is Rick's office. There's been some kind of accident—"

I drop the phone in my lap; downstairs, there's a loud concussion against the front door. Not someone knocking. More like someone throwing himself against the door. The crack and tinkle of broken windowpanes.

From the receiver on my lap, from the guy downstairs, I hear the same words, two different voices intertwining, saying the same thing.

Tom! Tom! You there?

BLOOD GIRL
JAAP BOEKESTEIN

Endless identical corridors, soft carpet which muted her high heels. Why did all these hotels, no matter where, look the same?

Nicole didn't wonder anymore. Her phone had told her the money was in her account and in which room she was expected. Those were the only things that mattered. After tonight she would be on the plane home, to recuperate until the next request.

Call girl.

She smiled. In a way she was.

Number 1246, the room. It was one of the bigger suites. The vamps always went for suites. Nothing cheap. Never.

The door opened before she had a chance to knock. They had heard her coming, in spite of the soft carpet. Vamp senses. They could hear a pin drop at a party. Or at least, one of night crawlers had once told her so.

It was five of them. Three males, two females. They looked human enough, unless you knew what to look for: a wax like shine on the skin, small faces, eyes that didn't blink often enough. And fangs of course, but normally they didn't show those.

She was the only human in the room. The only one with hot blood.

Three of them she had seen before, one female and one male were new faces.

They didn't waste time. They all knew the rules. They had all signed the standard agreement. It was just business. Money for services rendered.

In the middle of the room Nicole undressed. The five watched her like cats observing a little bird.

Skirt: it dropped and Nicole stepped out of the garment.

Blouse: a few quick buttons. She threw it on one the chairs.

If the vamps had tails, they all would be now stiff, swaying in union. Instead some of them licked their dry lips. Others had their mouth open. Fangs were showing, with all of them.

Nicole didn't wear any stockings. It just took too long to get out of them and leaving them on ruined them for sure. She had given up on stockings after a few times.

Her bra. Unhooked, thrown aside. She had a full bosom, nice nipples.

They were watching her. Oh, how they were watching her.

She paused to smile, playing with them. Old instincts, the beast inside them. They wanted to jump her, dig their nails and fangs in her flesh, tear open her veins.

Sure they wanted that. Oh yes.

But they wouldn't.

Nope.

Nowadays it was voluntarily—or paid—donors. Regulated, civilized. Rules, medical checks, the works.

Them vamps weren't allowed to do a thing, and Nicole knew it.

She smiled some more, looked every one of them in the eyes.

I know what you want. But you can't. No, you can't.

They liked that. They did. They liked to be challenged, to be teased, they liked to rub against the edges.

Nicole was wet by now. The anticipation made her wet. She knew they could smell her. That her lust was real. That was why she could make a living from it, and why so many other humans failed. Vamps didn't turn them on. It scared them or filled them with revulsion. They tried to fake it, but you couldn't fake with vamps. Never, ever.

In a way vamps were extremely honest.

She kicked away her heels. Now she was only wearing her panties. The thin ivory-colored piece of lace was her last protection.

One of the vamps, the new female—long blond hair, green eyes, a thin, regal nose—almost moved, *almost* rose. She froze in the very first millisecond and sat down again.

All the other vamps looked at her. So quickly Nicole would have missed it when she had blinked.

Oh oh, a faux pas.

Vamps were big on control. Self-control nowadays. The blond female vamp had just committed a sin equivalent to farting in public. Very embarrassing.

Newbie. Bag fed. Never tasted the real thing before?

Nicole hooked her thumbs behind the thin lace straps, wriggled with her ass and let her last undergarment drop. She knew what was coming and her body knew it too. Her breathing had quickened, her lips were dry and between her legs she felt the shimmering of anticipation. *Come and get it, suckers.*

They moved like a wave.

One moment they were sitting and standing, the next moment they were all over her. In one fluid motion she was half carried, half thrown on the king-size bed. Nicole landed soft as a feather, but she couldn't care less. Hands, nails, lips, tongues... She was touched in a dozen of spots in a dozen of different ways. They tasted her skin, smelled her, caressed, squeezed, tickled. One of the men was holding her head, oh so delicately, making sure his extended nails didn't hurt her. Hands on her back and buttocks. Kisses on her belly, one of the women. Soft strokes under her feet and at the inside of her elbows. Cheeks grazing her calves. Long, razor sharp nails running very lightly over her sensitive breasts. Skin on skin, flesh on flesh, a thousand sensations pulling her down in a sea of lust. One crawling mass of lovers focusing all their attention on her.

Vamps were the fucking best lovers in the world. No human could hold a candle to them. And that was why she loved what she did. Being used by a group of the hottest sex-machines in the world and being paid for it! Shit, life was good!

She was a pebble in tsunami, a mote of dust in a whirlwind. Flesh and lust everywhere. They didn't need to get into the mood, or get her into the mood. They all wanted it, now and hard and forever.

One of the males slid in her and started to fuck her while the two other males and the new female kept stimulating her body in every possible way. The female vamp who had been kissing Nicole's belly, now kissed her on the mouth.

Tongue on tongue, Nicole felt the vamp's fangs. The pupils of the female vamp were shrinking to pinpricks, a sure sign she was about to bite.

Do it bitch, do it! Nicole signaled her. To challenge the vamp she buried her own, human, teeth in the lip of the female.

Oh! The female vamp didn't like that! A human biting *her*? The response was swift and brutal; she tore herself loose and buried her fangs in Nicole's jugular.

Oh, fuck God! Yessssss! With a bite a vamp injected the prey with a whole bunch of natural drugs to pacify the victim. Being bitten by a vamp while being gangbanged at the same time was the fucking best feeling ever.

Nicole came. She was a slut, she knew it, she came quite easily. She loved coming. She loved vamps. She loved her fucking job!

Fangs in the flesh of her throat. Nicole could actually feel the teeth moving under her skin. It felt very wrong—a predator tearing your throat—and at the same time it was the best feeling ever.

Shit, shit...Yes! Go on!

With a satisfied growl the female vamp tore loose, making sure the wound was sealed with her healing saliva.

Nicole moaned. She wanted it to go on and on and on. She knew she was sex crazed, but she didn't care. *Fuck me, suck me, I am yours!*

The male vamp pulled out, his dick dripping wet from his and her cum. Sure, vamps came, but humans and vamp never made little half breeds. They were just too different.

The next male vamp took his turn, making Nicole lay face down with her ass in the air. Doggy style he entered her. One of the other males closed his mouth around Nicole's neck, not yet penetrating her flesh.

The male behind her pounded Nicole merciless while she buried her fists in the sheets of the bed. She moaned and drooled, not able to lift her head. The razor-sharp teeth held her neck and long, raw, cat-like tongue was crawling all over that spot where her spine begun. While a bunch of other hands and mouths were doing *most* evil things with the rest of her body.

"Bite me. Please bite me!" she begged. She was getting so hot. The vamp's dick reached all the right spots and she wanted to grind her ass against his body, but she couldn't move an inch.

Ow shittttttt! Two vamps were gently biting the palms of her hands, sending little lightings of lust through her body. One of the other vamps was playing with her breasts, massaging them rhythmically.

"Pleasssse," Nicole whimpered.

He bit. In her neck.

Her body shook, pushing it against the vamp fucking her from behind.

Orgasm avalanche...

She had died and gone to heaven. *It felt sooooooo good.*

Wow.

Wow!

Totally spaced out Nicole laid back on the bed, cushions supporting her head. The female vamp who had already drunk from her, cuddled her and gave her a kiss on the cheek. All other vamps were pleasing her flesh, gently, gently.

Nicole felt dizzy, but she knew it were her own body drugs and those of the vamps. The vamps actually drank very little and she could easily let a dozen feed on her. They just wanted the taste and the whole experience, not so much the nourishment. They had bags of blood, micro waved to the right temperature, for that.

The female vamp got down between Nicole's legs.

Oh fuck! On previous meetings the female vamp had also done that, and Nicole knew what to expect. She almost came by just remembering the whole thing.

Vamp lips closed around her soaked pussy. Tongue and teeth pushed them open. *Rough, sharp!*

The female vamp started to suck, while her inhuman long tongue slide into Nicole's hot cunt. The vamp's upper lip pushed against her clit, like had a life of their own.

Bitch, bitchbitchbitch...Wuhhhhh.

Nicole curved her back, opened her legs as far as possible, made little rocking movements with her pelvis just to feel more of the lips, tongue and teeth.

Two vamp mouths—the two males who hadn't fed yet— closed around her breasts. Gentle piercing ivory traps, holding her boobs. Sandpaper tongues curling around her rock-hard nipples.

*Oh God, no! Don't...Yes please. Fuck, yes please...*Nicole knew she wasn't very coherent anymore.

They teased her. The female vamp between her legs and the

two males sucking her breasts. But they only just had begun their torture.

Long nailed vamp fingers pried open Nicole's mouth. Glady she received a juicy, thick dick. She had to lean backwards to swallow the whole piece of vamp meat. Gently predator claws held her head while she deepthroated the whole thing.

Of course the three others kept doing their thing.

Isn't there five of them...?

Like djinn fulfilling her unspoken wish the fifth vamp, the new female, joined the delightful torture. Her long tongue slid between Nicole's firm buttocks to end right at that spot where the sun didn't shine. And after a quick circular motion, the female vamp's tongue entered her.

Owwwwwwwwwwwwwwww!

The five of them sucked and pushed and slithered and grinded and bit and...

Nicole was fucking dying from pleasure. Sensory overload. Her brains were surely frying! Her heart would certainly explode. The two tongues in her...*God.* The massive dick inside her mouth, tunneling itself in her throat, making her gasp for air. *Heaven.* And those two evil mouths sucking her tits. They-

The two vamps bit, sinking their teeth right at the same time in Nicole's breasts, opening veins.

Nicole rocked, came, kept coming.

She was drowning in orgasms, chocking on vamp flesh and cum. The fucker came, right in her throat, filling her. And those evil tongues...They were like electric eels, like jump starter cables kickstarting her body again and again and again.

Fuck.

...

...

Broken—happy, so happy—Nicole was laying in the bed, warm sweaty bodies under, up and against her. She had lost track of time, she barely knew she was alive. They had fucked her...Fucked her so good.

Shit, nobody fucked like vamps. She loved vamps. She wanted to be fucked by vamps forever.

The new female was watching her from two feet away, hunger in her eyes. She was the only one who hadn't fed yet. She had the lowest status. Vamps were very aware of status, of face. It had to do with age, and lineage and a bunch of other things Nicole couldn't remember right now. All had fed, now it was time for the newbie to feed.

The young female vamp wanted it. She wanted it so bad. She was hot and excited, everything smelled of blood and sweat and cum. A heady perfume. A hot, radiating, human body nearby. Her fangs and claws were out. Her pupils were little black dots.

She wanted it bad.

She slid towards Nicole.

On a whim Nicole pushed her away.

Frustrated the vamp tried again.

Nicole pushed her away once more, denying what the young vamp wanted most.

Uh uh! You got to work for it. You'll have to earn this, baby. I am no vamp, but I will lose face if I just give in.

The female vamp hissed, launched herself.

Nicole, who had been expecting that exact move, slid back, seeking protection from the other vamps who understood the whole dynamics of the situation.

I am theirs. Not yours.

The older female vamp put her arms around Nicole, hissed. The three males joined her. A protective cocoon of limbs.

The young female vamp growled, held back. She wanted... she wanted...How unfair! She had done everything with this human slut, she had waited her turn, she had showed respect to the others and now...now...She meowed like a little kitten.

Suddenly the protective vamp limbs around Nicole, tensed, became bound of flesh. Hands holding Nicole's arms behind her back. Legs capturing her legs, a hand in her hair, pulling her head backwards.

Nicole struggled, pro forma, but she knew it was utterly in vain. She couldn't fight a vamp. Let alone four.

She was caught, she was prey. No matter what she did, she couldn't escape.

She was getting wet all over again.

The four elder vamps offered her—prey—to the young one.

Nicole shivered, clenched her teeth, pretending to struggle. *Shit, this is so hot.*

After a millisecond of hesitation, the young female vamp jumped Nicole, buried her fangs in the throbbing artery of the captive human.

Nicole wasn't being fucked, but she came nonetheless when the female vamp drank from her. She had been fucked so thoroughly almost anything set her of.

With the last vamp feeding on her, Nicole surrendered. Powerful hands gripping her, her throat exposed. The only thing she could do was submit. No choice but to enjoy what was done to her. No shame, no guilt, just pleasure.

She...She is greedy...Her first time...

Nicole felt the how glow of the vampire's drugs spreading through her body.

She...keeps on drinking...when does she...stop?

A distant feeling of panic, blanketed by layers and layers of soothing natural chemicals, shouted at the back of Nicole's mind. *Stop! This...too much!*

Feeding frenzy. Nicole had heard the stories, but that was what they were: stories. Vampires didn't lose control. It just wasn't done.

But this newbie couldn't stop, her instincts had overwhelmed her.

She will drink me dry!

Wild panic flared through Nicole's body, but she was

completely unable to move a muscle.

I'll die!

Nicole's feet and arms started to sting.

The other vampires noticed something was wrong.

They tore the young female from Nicole's throat.

Nicole passed out, shaking with the most intense orgasm she had ever felt.

The vamps paid everything. The hospital bill, the money the penalty clause of the contract stipulated, a hefty extra sum, transport back home, flowers...

A vamp hadn't killed, or in this case *almost* killed, a human for over fifty years. It was national news and Nicole got sick of the press and all the attention real quick. Offers for exclusive interviews, movie deals, talk shows, support rallies and hate mail...She was glad when the cab dropped her off at her apartment building. It was late in the evening and nobody was waiting outside.

In the passageway, next to her front door, one was.

The blond female vamp with the green eyes and the regal nose. The one that almost sucked her dry. She was wearing a plain, long black dress, a bit monastic-like.

Nicole looked at the female. "What do you want?"

The vamp bowed, with downcast eyes she said: "My name is Laura. I apologize for my terrible behavior and the harm I've caused you. I've been sent here to do serve you."

Oh, shit. Vamps and their honor! They sent her to serve me? This is ultimate humiliation for a vamp: being submissive to a human. Nicole understood. Sending this female to her, was the vamp's way of saving face. Trying to wash away the enormous embarrassment this Laura had caused her species.

"Serve me? How? For how long? Look at me."

The female Laura looked up. Her green eyes flared. She wasn't happy at all.

"As long and anyway as you see fit."

"And what will happen if I refuse you?" *Like I want to have a vamp servant around.*

She didn't want to show it, but suddenly there was fear in the vamp's eyes.

"That means you won't accept the apologies and that I will have failed."

And failure isn't an option, is it? Nicole looked at the female vamp. She was young. Younger then Nicole. *What will they do if you fail? Banishment? Your name being stricken from the Books of Lineage? For a vamp that is a fate worse than death.*

Nicole took her keys from her purse and unlocked the door of her apartment. She smiled encouraging.

"Come in Laura, we will figure something out."

WHAT LURKS IN PARADISE?
WEASEL

He had Lucas tied down to the bed. The ropes were just tight enough to press against his pale body. Alex trailed a hand along his partner's soft belly before latching the nipple clamps. His darkened brown arm smoothed over freshly shaved flesh. He loved the feel when Lucas had just showered and shaved. The slick wetness of his body combined with the smoothness made him eager to play.

Alex smiled as Lucas let out a small moan beneath the gag as he tightened the clamp. Meticulously, he placed four pads on the boy's chest and turned on his e-stim remote. "You okay, babe?" He asked before turning on his device, his thumbs eager to shoot a few jolts into his submissive. Lucas nodded and Alex set the device to a medium pulse. His partner's body tightened, fighting the bindings that held him down as he was shocked along his torso. Alex watched for a moment, waiting to see any signals to stop before he cut off his boyfriend's underwear. Lucas moaned hard, his cock twitching beneath his sky-blue briefs.

Alex tried to settle his partner's body down, rubbing Lucas' belly as he slid a knife under the waist line and sliced upward, ripping the briefs flawlessly. He then rubbed the knife along his partner's thigh, causing Lucas to moan louder beneath his gag. His cock flailed consistently, like a heartbeat working its hardest. The knife left Lucas' thigh as Alex leaned forward and engulfed his boyfriend's cock, the knife resting now on Lucas' nipple.

He was a brown blur, sliding along the throbbing shaft quick, his teeth only lightly grazing the tip. Alex could taste the pre leaking into his mouth causing his tongue to lick around the shaft as he continued to work.

Lucas released a series of moans, his body attacked by shocks and Alex's mouth, sensations his body hadn't felt in a long time. His mind tried escaping to slow his orgasm down, but his body kept it right in the moment. It wasn't long before he shot his load into his boyfriend's mouth.

Alex swallowed everything that entered, then positioned himself between Lucas' legs. He held them high as he lubed and pressed his cock against his submissive's hole. Before he could thrust himself in, the front door shut. Alex looked over his shoulder, confused at what he just heard. Then amidst the silence a voice shot out. "Babe, I'm home. God you won't believe what happened at chorus today. Those fuckwits!"

He looked back at his boyfriend, questions tumbling around in his skull like broken glass on sheet metal. Alex looked back over his shoulder and saw another Lucas standing behind him, mouth agape at what he was seeing.

"What the actual fuck!" Alex said as he pushed away and cornered himself against the dresser. Before the new Lucas could say anything, the bound boyfriend started to shake violently. Alex's attention turned to see the bindings break loose as the bound partner started to shift, his eyes becoming fierce, crazed. He couldn't understand it. He looked back at the bedroom door and the man standing there seemed shaken.

The man had his hand against his mouth, frozen by the

transformation happening. A monster started to form, flesh stretching thin across bone, claws at the edges of its fingers.

Alex made a quick decision and jumped to the real Lucas, "Babe we gotta go,now!" he said pushing him out of the door. Before Alex could reach the kitchen, the creature grabbed him, his claws digging right through his chest. Blood splattered across and all over Lucas' face. He couldn't even think to scream, grabbing a knife to protect himself. The beast grunted, his free claw twisting Alex's head off his body like a twist off beer bottle. It drank whatever blood spewed from his neck before throwing the body to the side and going after Lucas.

"Leave me alone!" Lucas screamed as he ran into the living room of his apartment. The beast blocking the door, his only escape was to break the window. Lucas threw his knife and made a run for the large glass behind him, hoping to burst right through. His hand reached out, touching the glass as the beast grabbed him by his foot. Lucas was dragged back to the monster, forced to look over the creature's face. A deformed skull hung over him, stretched pale flesh seemed as if it were about to rip open. He didn't know what to do, he kicked up, the beast biting his leg as he did so.

Lucas screamed as the monster's teeth ripped through his bone. He tried to crawl away, but he was still caught, forced to sit and listen to the crunch of his bones being obliterated by the beast in his home. He took one last look at it, it's large open eyes, ragged jaw, and emotionless expression. He screamed as he shot up and tried punching it, only falling right into the mouth of the creature.

The sun was setting outside as the beast devoured the body, chewing it slowly, meticulously. It wanted to crunch every little bone its dinner had. When he finished, he grabbed Alex's corpse and started to eat, filling the apartment with a loud, booming crunch.

DRAINAGE
JONATHAN W. THURSTON

May 1, 2020

"Hey, Daryl, how are you holding up?" the officer says as he walks in.

Daryl knows the drill at this point. It had been the sixth time this officer had been over in the past month. He lets the officer in, just wearing a tank top and short shorts. "As well as I can be," he says. Daryl's face is far from pale, but his eyes seem glazed over, his cheeks sunken in, his face bearing a goatee and scruff along his cheeks and neck. "Want a cup of coffee, Officer Kurt?"

"Sure, don't mind if I do," the officer says, closing the door behind him and walking into the apartment.

Walking into the kitchen, Daryl gets a coffee mug down from the cabinet and starts fixing a cup for Officer Kurt. "No word, I'm assuming?" Daryl asks softly, not wanting to raise his head.

The officer lowers his hat. "No, son. We haven't heard a thing yet. The chief wanted me to ask you a few last questions, and then we will leave you alone until we have a lead."

Daryl tried to hold the tears back. Lorenzo had been gone

for almost a full month now. No one knew where he had gone off to. No one knew what had happened. Daryl's fiancé hadn't used his credit cards. He hadn't taken his car. He was just... gone. Of course, the cops had interrogated him most heavily at first. But now that they knew he wasn't responsible for Lorenzo's disappearance, they had been working together to try to find out what had happened. "Sure, ask away, Kurt." He handed the officer the mug and sat down on the couch opposite the muscular cop.

"Ok, so we know the last you heard of him was the last night he was here—"

"Yep. As I've said, we were curled up in bed, right back there. I had just finished reading, and he was snoring something awful. I went to sleep. When I woke up, he was gone." It was only the fifth time Daryl had had to say it. It was annoying the second and third time. Now, it was just going through the motions though.

"I know you've said he wouldn't have any enemies here or even any family here. Do you...Do you think he might have... gone off with someone else?"

Daryl froze. The thought had crossed his mind once or twice, what if Lorenzo *had* gone off to elope with someone else? "I've thought about it. But I just don't think so. He's an independent guy. He wouldn't want to just be taken care of by someone else. Unless you've noticed any credit card use?"

The cop shook his head and sipped his coffee. "Nah. Nothing like that...Mind if I use your bathroom real quick? Sorry, have been on the road all morning."

"Not at all; go for it. Just finished the renovations yesterday. Mind if I work on my woodcraft stuff here?"

"Hey, it's your house."

"Cool." Daryl pulled the little wooden figurine off the shelf beside the couch and opened the can of varnish on the coffee table. He dipped a brush in, and just as he began to work the varnish into the wood, he heard the officer call from the bathroom:

"Hey, how's this thing work?"

Daryl smiled. He had just installed a Japanese toilet in the bathroom. He missed his time in Japan—the one month he had spent there—and had made a lot of changes around the house since Lorenzo had vanished, his own kind of coping mechanism. "You just squat and go, officer."

He heard a loud groan from the officer and then, "'kay."

Daryl kept working on his wood project for the next several minutes, careful not to get any varnish on his fingers. That stuff was a bitch to get out.

He had really taken up a number of old hobbies the past month. He'd picked up the clarinet again. He'd redone the whole bathroom. He started woodworking again. Even got into playing online Go. And yet, there was no sign that Lorenzo was ever going to come back.

He heard the fan come on in the bathroom as the officer came back into the living room. "Sorry about that," the officer started. "Been having stomach issues."

"Hope it wasn't the coffee!" Daryl said with concern. He knew Officer Kurt had only had a couple sips, but still...

"Nah. Just last night's dinner not agreeing with me." Daryl gestured for the officer to have a seat, but Officer Kurt just shook his head. "Nah, I'd best be going. I didn't figure you'd have anything new to tell me. This was more just a going-by-the-books visit. Still, you know how to reach me, yeah?"

Daryl nodded.

"Alright, well take care. And..." the officer started as he opened the door to the apartment building hallway, "I'm really sorry."

Daryl smiled weakly and just said, "Thanks."

That night, as Daryl fucked himself mechanically with a dildo, he tried to imagine his fiancé's thrusts. He tried to mimic the pattern. *Slow, slow, slow.* Then a few seconds of *fast, fast, fast.* But it just wasn't the same. He didn't cum that night. And as he lay there, curling up in a fetal position, he could almost envision his fiancé lying right there with him, snoring against him. For the past year, that snoring had grated on him, annoyed him. But now...he kinda missed it.

He closed his eyes to sleep, vaguely remembering he should close the blinds over the bedroom window a bit tighter since they were half-open but ultimately deciding he didn't care. If anyone was watching him, let them.

May 2, 2020

The next morning, Daryl stretched, took a piss in his new toilet, started a pot of coffee, and checked on the varnish of his woodwork. Still needed to dry a bit, but not much longer. He went through all his morning routines, all his new ones anyway. Life without Lorenzo was different...quieter. Unsettlingly quiet.

He knew the cops wouldn't come by today, not unless they suddenly had something new on the case. And that seemed unlikely at this point.

When the coffee finally reached his bowels, he went to the bathroom, squatted over the Japanese toilet and pulled out his phone. He started Googling "Lorenzo Bates." When that came up with a rugby player in Brazil, he rolled his eyes and added the word "Michigan" to his search. That's when the search results became relevant.

There were a good ten to fifteen news articles from throughout the past month. Most of them were small, just stating that Lorenzo was a guy who had gone missing. A couple of them made a bit more of a story out of it: gay guy moves up to Michigan, gets engaged, and then disappears. As if the three events were connected. Daryl rolled his eyes again. One story from a conservative news site speculated that Daryl himself had something to do with it and that the cops did not investigate thoroughly enough.

"Assholes," Daryl said, punctuating the word with a plop in the toilet. "Fucking assholes." He wished the news outlets would try to get people to turn information forward or paint Lorenzo in a more positive light than just "missing victim." It was heartbreaking. It really was.

Later that day, Daryl's phone went off. His heart leaped. When he looked down, he saw it said "Tanner." That was Lorenzo's sibling's name. He answered immediately: "Hey."

"Hey," Tanner responded. "No news, I'm guessing?"

Daryl was silent and looked down at his feet.

"It's ok. I figured as much. Look, I...I wanted to tell you... Mom's planning a funeral."

"What? But we don't...have a...body...yet," Daryl said, struggling with the words.

"I know. I tried telling her not to, but you know how she is by now. So, she's doing it. I don't have any details yet, but when they happen, I'd like you to come. If that's alright?"

"Yeah, yeah, of course," Daryl said softly. "Of course."

"Thanks, Daryl. It'll mean a lot to me. And Mom would like it too, even if she won't say she would."

"Ok." They were silent for a whole minute after that, and when Daryl looked at his phone, he saw they had hung up. He sighed and put the phone down.

Later on, he felt frustrated. At everything. The police. The news. Lorenzo's family. Lorenzo even. While Daryl was a bottom, he suddenly felt the need to just *fuck* something. So, he did what most people who lived alone did: he made do with what he had. He took his shorts off, walked to the bathroom, crouched over the pristine, chrome toilet and started fucking the drain. This drain wasn't hard or sharp-edged like many pipes. It was softer than that. All he needed to do was crouch down—in an admittedly uncomfortable position, even for him—lube up, and stick it in the hole. He fucked it as hard as he could without hurting himself, eyes and jaw clenching, and came hard down the drain. He gasped out and tried not to cry. He stayed there for a minute, letting the frustration wash away from him.

Then, he heard a sharp sound. It sounded like a snort or cough. Falling back, he jumped to his feet and left the bathroom, checking to see if someone was in the apartment with him. "Officer Kurt?" he called into the mostly dark apartment.

No answer.

Nervously, he went and turned the bathroom light off, went to his bedroom, closed the door, locked it, and crawled into bed.

Rain started outside.

And as he closed his eyes, he thought he heard something. He thought he heard snoring.

May 3, 2020

In the afternoon, Daryl had to deal the mess he made the previous day. His little toilet-fucking had let to a major clog in the toilet. "This," he started talking to himself, "this right here is why I always let Lorenzo handle the manly stuff. Who was I kidding thinking I could make this a functional toilet? Keeps stopping up." It didn't help that Daryl also did not have a plunger. Or common sense. Book smarts, he had plenty. Common sense, not so much. And that's how he proceeded to try to unclog the toilet but pushing a large dildo in and out of it. It occasionally made large sucking sounds. Suction was happening. But the clog took the better part of an hour to clear up.

As he was wrapping that up, Tanner called again.

"Yes?" Daryl said, more frustrated than he had been yesterday.

"Oh, sorry, is this a bad time?"

"No, no, you're fine. Just having a...draining day."

"I get that. I'm sorry. Look, Mom sent me the details for the funeral. It's supposed to happen in a couple of weeks."

"Damn, so soon?"

"Yeah..." Tanner said sadly. "But look, I'll help pay for your plane ticket."

Daryl's eyes widened for a moment. "Really? You want to help that much?" It seemed a bit suspicious to Daryl. A bit too friendly. He had always gotten along with Tanner, but Tanner had never invited to help out like this so personally. Keeping the phone to his ear, Daryl walked to the window and looked out the blinds. A person was walking their dog along the adjacent sidewalk. Cars drove by here and there. Yet, he suddenly felt like he was being watched.

"Of course I do. You were...you were gonna be my brother-in-law. I do care about you."

Daryl sighed. "Okay. I'm interested. Text me the time and date specifics and I'll check out flights."

It took Daryl the better part of the evening to get it sorted out, and he went to bed early than usual. The rain had kept him up much of the night before. But tonight wouldn't be much better. Even though there was no rain, as soon as he lay in bed, he heard it, and it was for sure this time, crystal clear: snoring. It sounded like it was coming from right beside him. No, it felt like it was echoing all around the room. All around him as he tried to sleep. He pulled a pillow over his head and tried to block his ears. But the snoring continued.

zzz...

ZZZZZ....

zzz...

ZZZZZ...

May 4, 2020

He wasn't able to even get to sleep until dawn, when his eyes had become bloodshot and the pillowcase tear-stained. While he slept, he missed three calls from Tanner. A newspaper reporter emailed him asking for an interview. Daryl's own mom texted him to check up on him. And the postwoman dropped off a book package at the door. But all of this Daryl ignored. He just wanted sleep. He felt like he was going crazy from hearing the snoring all night.

He woke up still not well rested and horny to boot. Without even leaving bed, he grabbed the dildo. It looked just like Lorenzo's had: medium size, bulging near the top, and the slightest curve downward. "Please just fuck me," Daryl pleaded to the air. "Quit haunting me with your snores. Please." He pushed the dildo inside him over and over, the other hand pumping his own dick. He just wanted to cum and go back to sleep.

But suddenly he felt a sensation all too unexpected. Warmth. Liquid warmth. The dildo was cumming in his ass. "What the fuck?!" he yelled and pulled the now throbbing dildo out of his ass. He looked at it in disbelief and saw Lorenzo's veins throbbing. "That's impossible," he said, throwing the varnished, amputated penis across the room. "That's fucking impossible."

In response, he heard snores.

It wasn't just the steady snores from last night. It was like multiple layers of snores, different volumes. Different tones. All around him. Directly in his ears. Over and over. Some sputtering and fast. Some long and drawn out, rising in volume as they went.

He clamped his hands to his ears and screamed. "*Fuuuuuuck!*" But the snores didn't abate.

He ran to the bathroom and fell onto the tiles. The snores were loudest here. They echoed off the walls. Echoed off the tiles. And they all came from the hole in the drain.

Daryl put his face up to the drain and cried. "I'm sorry. I'm sorry. I couldn't handle it. I couldn't handle it anymore. Night after night. After night. After night. I couldn't handle it."

He tried working his fingers under the metal lip of the toilet, trying to unearth it from the floor, remove it from his lover's open frozen mouth that was the drain, but it was glued on tight. He had done a better job than he thought.

"Please! Please just stop the snoring! Please, baby. I'll do anything. Please!!!"

The snoring kept going.

Daryl couldn't take it. He threw open the closet door and grabbed the container of bleach. "I'll join you, baby. I'll join you the way I made you go!" The lip of the bottle still tasted like Lorenzo's lips when Daryl had forcefed his fiancé the bottle. And now, Daryl chugged the poisonous liquid hungrily. Begging the noise to stop.

ZZZZZ...

zzz...

ZZZZZZZZ...

zzzzz...

ZZZZZZZZZZZZZZ....

May 5, 2020

That same time the next day, cops had infested the apartment. What they found shocked all of them, especially Officer Kurt. In the bedroom, they found Lorenzo's dick, kept erect with a thick layer of polyurethane and sticky with lube. In the bathroom, Daryl's naked body had blood and bleach leaking out of most of his orifices, sprawled out in front of the toilet.

But a spatter of vomit in the toilet gave the police some pause: it wasn't Daryl's. And when they unearthed the new Japanese-style toilet, they found the body of Lorenzo Bates. He had been bound; his ass had been plugged with a toy with superglue; his jaw had been forced open with an O-ring gag; his tongue had been cut out, as had his vocal cords; and his time of death? The coroners were suspecting it had been only a couple of hours after Daryl's.

Officer Kurt vomited when he realized what he had done.

The police had come after being called by Daryl and Lorenzo's neighbors. Early that morning, they called to report weird sounds coming from the neighboring room. It sounded like snoring.

BIOGRAPHIES

YSADORA ALEXANDER is an eclectic writer, artist and professional witch from Perth, Western Australia. When not immersed in zine culture, as a writer and editor for both Femme Politika and The Pagan Press, Ysadora writes disturbing short stories in the horror genre. They are currently completing a series of novels in the New Adult paranormal romance genre, which will be decidedly less disturbing.

MIKE BENDZELA'S work has appeared in many journals and anthologies, including *The Pushcart Prize XVIII* and *MEN ON MEN 7*. His experimental erotic novella, "February," has been published in Running Wild Press's Novella Anthology. A book of short tales, "Metazoan Variations: Evolutionary Fables and Other Emblematic Tales," is forthcoming from UnCollected Press. He lives with his husband on a farm in Maine.

JAAP BOEKESTEIN (1968) is an award winning Dutch writer of science fiction, fantasy, horror, thrillers and whatever takes his fancy. Five novels and almost three hundred of his stories have been published. His has made his living as a bouncer, working for a detective agency and as editor.

WILLIAM HOLDEN'S has been writing for over twenty-two years with over 130 published short stories, novellas, and books. He is an award-winning author and four-time Lambda Literary Award Finalist. www.williamholdenwrites.com
>   *A Twist of Grimm* - Lethe Press, 2010 (Lambda Literary Finalist)
>   *Words to Die By* - Bold Stroke Books, 2012 (2nd place Rainbow Book Awards for best horror)
>   *Secret Societies* – Bold Stroke Books, 2012 (Lambda Literary Finalist)

The Thief Taker – Bold Strokes Books, 2014 (Lambda Literary Finalist)
Grave Desires – Lethe Press, 2015 (Lambda Literary Finalist)
Crimson Souls – Bold Strokes Books (2016).

LIA MEYERS is the pen name of a nonbinary lesbian graduate student and novelist from the NYC area.

JAKE NEVILLE is twenty-one year old writer-director of primarily filmic work, residing in Melbourne, Australia. With a queer eye, Jake's stories always feature prominent LGBTQ+ themes and characters that strive to break the mold. His stories also tend to examine the fine line between the ugly and the beautiful.

JONATHAN W. THURSTON is an editor for Sinister Stoat Press. They like both bodies and blood. He's got HIV. These things are not related.

WEASEL is a queer author and The Dude of Weasel Press. His latest book, *Cut the Loss*, was released July 2019. His short horror collection *Carnage* is set to release October 2020.

TAMARA WERTEEN lives in sunny Florida with her wife and children. By day she wears the title of nurse, and by night she pens dark tales of bad things happening to good people. She has published her first horror anthology, *Bump in the Night*, and has short works included in *Death and Beetles* and *Horror USA: Washington*, all available on Amazon.com

OTHER TITLES FROM SINISTER STOAT PRESS

The City Around the World by Elliot Harper

The Last Book You'll Ever Read by Scott Hughes

The Devil has a Black Dog by Jonathan W. Thurston

Dread edited by Weasel

The Haunted Traveler edited by Weasel

Ghostly Pornographers by Thomas White

COMING SOON TO SINISTER STOAT PRESS

Spiders in our Bed by Jonathan W. Thurston

Carnage by Weasel

DARK TITLES FROM WEASEL PRESS
& RED FERRET PRESS

POETRY

Pan's Saxophone by Jonel Abellanosa
The Madness of Empty Spaces by David E. Cowen
The Seven Yards of Sorrow by David E. Cowen
Bleeding Saffron by David E. Cowen
Face Down in the Leaves by Dwale
Satan's Sweethearts by Marge Simon and Mary Turzillo
Wolf: An Epic and Other Poems by Z.M. Wise

FICTION

City, Psychonaut by Robin Wyatt Dunn
Dark is a Color of the Day by Robin Wyatt Dunn
Brinwood by RK Gold
The Goat: Building the Perfect Victim by Bill Kieffer
In and of Blood by Kat Lewis
Viscera by Manna Plourde
Taxi Sam in PINK NOIR by Neil S. Reddy
Not Kafka: A Collection of Ugly Shorts by Neil S. Reddy
Tales in Liquid Time by Neil S. Reddy